The Return Of Benjamin Quincy

A Rosewood Novel

~*~

Susan Lute

Crazy Hair Publishing
Portland, OR

Susan Lute

Published by Susan Lute
Crazy Hair Publishing
www.susanlute.com

Book Layout Crazy Hair Publishing
The Return Of Benjamin Quincy -- 1st ed. by Susan Lute

This book is dedicated to Darla, Ginger, and Wendy. They are the ones who told me they would hunt me to the ends of the earth before they would let me go.

ONE

*S*he let herself into her boss' house – almost ex-boss now – gleefully rubbing her mental hands together like a woman who'd just discovered the perfect Prada handbag on the seventy-five percent sale rack. Not that a Prada bag worth its salt would allow itself to be found in a little town where the highlights of the week were JV and Varsity football, but Sydney Marshall was forever optimistic.

When her father was alive, he'd taken her to the football games from the time she was a little girl. She missed those times, when the banter was all about which player was going to take the home team to the playoffs.

Her father had taught her that life was magical, but the magic had died with him, and since she'd dragged her feet long enough, now it was time to make some magic of her own. Finally, after spending the last eleven years working for Meredith, first as her girl Friday, then operating the presses while she went to school getting her journalism degree, and finally making her mark as a local travel writer, she was more than ready to spread her wings.

She had the job, the plane ticket and a studio apartment waiting in Manhattan. All that was left was get on that plane, which she had every intention of doing, as soon as she tied up the last of her loose ends.

Closing the door behind her, Syd eased into the room packed to the brim with people she'd known all her life. The volume was loud. The scent of newly baked cinnamon rolls made her mouth water.

In all the excitement of clearing out her desk at *The Rosewood Gazette* and locking the door of Rosewood's only newspaper behind her for the last time, she'd forgotten breakfast. The warm smell of gooey pastries drew her to the kitchen. She would miss Ester Reed's sinful confections. No one made pastries like Grant's grandma.

And speak of the devil. Her best friend since he came to town to help his grandmother run Rose's Bakery grabbed her and spun her in tight circles as though she were nine instead of twenty-nine. "Are you packed?"

"Almost. Put me down, you lug."

"Knew it. Two weeks to go and you probably have all those boxes you had me drag to your place packed, triple taped shut, and stacked in alphabetical order."

Grinning, 'cause Grant wasn't far off the mark, she slapped his shoulder. "I'm not that bad."

Her feet dropped to the floor.

"Really? Could have fooled me. How did game night go last night? Sorry I couldn't make it."

"As usual. Delle Burns won again."

"She is one lucky lady."

As a clothes concept, subtlety was lost on Grant. Today he had on a bright red shirt he'd gotten at a Star Trek convention. It clashed painfully with the pea-green cargo pants he'd paired it with.

Wincing, Syd shielded her eyes in mock horror. "What is that you're wearing?"

"What? What's wrong with my clothes?" His blonde, thick hair was pulled into a short tail at the back of his neck. Blue eyes twinkled merrily at her. "Who's going to eat my cooking when you're gone?"

"The usual. Everyone in town who's not bedridden." She punched his arm and added hopefully, "If you get lonely you can always come see me in New York. You'll cook. I'll eat. It'll be like old times."

He snorted. "Hardly."

"I'm looking for Meredith. I have to give her the keys to the office."

Grant turned uncharacteristically serious. "Are you sure you really want to move clear across the country?"

"Positive. Haven't you heard? The center of the universe is New York City." Syd let her grin grow, cocky and a little full of herself. "And I couldn't ask for a better opportunity. Can you imagine writing for *The Traveler*?"

"Well no. Not my thing," Grant smirked. "Meredith's in her office. Said she had a call to make."

Syd rose on her toes and kissed his cheek. What would she have done without him when her world was falling apart, and all the years since? "I'll text."

"You bet your pretty ass you will."

Laughing, she threaded her way through the crowded living room.

"Congratulations on your new job, Sydney."

"Thanks, Henry."

Henry was owner and chief mechanic of the one auto shop in town, Henry's Auto Repair. When she got on the plane, her beloved cherry-red VW would be parked in his parking lot, a *For Sale* sign displayed prominently in the window.

Velma Caldwell stopped her with a tentative touch on her arm. "I wish *I* was brave enough to sell all my things and move clear across the country."

Syd bit the inside of her cheek. Everyone knew, you-know-where would have to freeze over before Velma, Rosewood's head librarian, would leave her post.

"I was told Meredith is in her office. Have you seen her?"

Velma shook her head, "Sorry."

More well wishes and congratulations kept her from making speedy work of running Meredith to ground. Her ex-boss ran *The Gazette* from the office she'd set up in a spare room a few years ago, after which she'd insisted Syd take over the publisher's office at the Main Street building. It was an ongoing game played – by those who would remain unnamed, Syd mocked herself – to keep her in town. *Bribe the kid, so she'll stay close to home.*

But in the end, she'd won. Her feet did a little happy dance.

There had been a time – God, how long ago it seemed – when she'd dreamed of sharing a sparkling, big life with the handsomest, smartest boy in school. They'd planned a lifetime together. But her dad had gotten cancer, and everything after that had changed.

She swallowed the sneaky remnant of grief, and slashed aside the memory of the last time she'd seen Benjamin Quincy. She was moving on. Ten years too late. But moving on, just as he had.

Pulling the keys from her pocket, she stepped into Meredith's office. The room was neat as a pin, as usual. The phone was off the hook, but the woman who'd given her the refuge she no longer needed wasn't there.

Frowning, Syd stepped around the desk to hang up the phone. With a gasp, she came up short, her hand flying to her mouth. A squeak of horror escaped between her fingers as she dropped to her knees beside the still body. "Meredith!"

The older woman lay twisted partially onto her back, eyes closed, skin pale, her breathing shallow. She moaned.

"Meredith?" Syd picked up the out-flung hand and felt for a pulse. "Help! Someone help!

~*~

"I don't want to live here. I want to go live with Mom." Isabel's wail ended in the too familiar sound of stomping feet.

Ben wanted her to be happy, but he didn't dare let his daughter see how easily she could scored points off her old man. Solely responsible for her now, he wasn't about to give in because being a good dad was the hardest thing he'd ever tackled.

A gamin face snuck into his thoughts. Riotous blonde curls kissed with sunlight framed clear topaz eyes. It took him back almost a dozen years. Ben swore under his breath. It was inevitable that coming back to the scene of his own happy childhood would resurrect the memories he'd buried of his high school girlfriend.

Sydney Marshall should be long gone from Rosewood. It was all she'd ever talked about – until the day her dad was diagnosed with bone cancer.

Forget her. You have more important fish to fry. Not the easiest advise to follow. Never had been.

"Daaad! You're not listening."

"Of course I am. Go check out the upstairs. You can't tell me you don't like the house until you've seen the whole thing."

Isabel huffed out a breath on a high dramatic note, but did as she was told. Her shoulders slumped as she dragged her feet up the stairs. The toes of her shoes caught each riser, leaving behind a rhythmic hollow clunk.

Despite his efforts to push Sydney's image out of his mind, along with the way she'd heartlessly cast him out of her life, he could still hear the tinkle of her laughter. Thinking Isabel hardly ever laughed, he buried the offending memory. Again.

Stay focused, Quincy.

He went through the rest of the first floor with an eye to what improvements needed to be done before they could move in. The craftsman style bungalow needed work, but at a glance it looked like he should be able to do most of it himself.

Isabel needed this. *He* needed this. He couldn't fail his daughter again, the way he had when he'd mistakenly let Diana take her to New York, thinking a child should be with its mother.

Listening to her footsteps moving from room to room above his head, he found the realtor, Robin Weston, a sultry brunette, with a teasing wink and wicked smile aimed directly at him, in the kitchen.

He considered her unspoken offer. Dating a local girl. Could work. Perhaps later, when his pride didn't feel quite so bruised. Two blunders in the female department wasn't the best track record for a single dad. "How long will it take to close on the house?"

"Not long at all. Mrs. Frank is quite happy with your offer," Robin all but purred. "I hear you're getting *The Gazette*, too. Meredith must be so relieved you're buying it. It's been a financial burden for her for a long time, and now, with her recent illness and Sydney Marshall moving to New York–"

His brows slammed together. "I'm sorry, Mrs. Frank is sick?"

"You haven't heard? Well. I'm sorry to be the bearer of bad news. Meredith had a stroke three days ago."

Three days ago he'd been on the road with Isabel. Before he'd left Chicago, he'd made arrangements to have lunch with Meredith – he glanced at his watch – in an hour to sign papers and finalize their agreement to partner for the first year while he got his feet underneath him.

Disturbed by the news and worried for the older woman he'd been dealing with by phone for the last three months, he gave Robin his cell number, then eased her out of the house.

He'd grown fond of Meredith. Respected her long business experience. Her ill health was unexpected, but he would untangle the legal ramifications after he saw her. Unless *The Gazette* was in bankruptcy, he saw no reason to change his plans at this juncture.

Anxious to check on his soon-to-be business partner, he took the stairs two at a time, making it to the second floor before it percolated what else Robin had said.

Sydney Marshall was moving to New York. Sydney was still in Rosewood? The world stood still until he found his daughter in one of the rooms that opened off the landing.

Isabel. She was the one who mattered now. Shoulders slumped, she stood at a window overlooking the town. It'd started to rain; a soft, reassuring patter on the roof. In the diffused light, the ten year old watched cars moving lazily along the wet streets below.

Ben's heart skipped. His girl spent way too much of her time watching and not doing. "I told the Real Estate lady we'd take the house."

Isabel's chin drooped to her chest. "Mom's not going to let me live with her, is she?"

He could do this. He could be a good dad. Half the problem was his kid was too smart for her own good. He shoved a hand in his pocket and crossed his fingers. The musty smell of the empty house enveloped him. "No Baby, she's not."

She squeezed her eyes in an effort to hold back tears. His heart pinched st her bravery.

Voice wobbling, she exhaled softly. "You could talk to her. Make her–"

He dropped to his knees, drawing his darling girl into his arms. Her trembling frame was too fragile, so he told a bad lie mixed with most of the truth. "I would. If I thought it was best for you to be with your mom. But I think it's better you stay with me."

How could he make his child understand, while living in the shadow of her mother's career, Isabel had become a ghost in Diana's life? "Is it such a terrible thing, living with your old man?"

Isabel sniffled against his shoulder. "I guess not."

His heart turned to mush, as it always did where his baby was concerned. He dug out his handkerchief and handed it over. "You'll like it here, I promise."

She was quiet for a long minute, while she scrubbed at her eyes. "I like this room."

Relief whooshed out of his chest. First hurtle overcome. "It's yours then."

"I won't fit in."

He knuckled the top of her head. "You will."

"I wish I was pretty enough to be a model. Then I could go to Paris on my own. And to London and Tokyo and Rio." All places Diana talked of; a dream instilled by his ex-wife's obsession with her fashion career and overlaid with a ten-year-old's wistful desire for her mother's attention. "Everyone would love me and beg me to wear their cloths."

One step forward, two steps back. "How about you be a

kid awhile longer. You can become a world famous model when you're thirty."

Isabel reared back, the look on her sweet face horrified. "Daaad. That's like forever!"

He stood, smothering a chuckle. All he had to say to that was, "Thank goodness."

Their steps down the stairs echoed in the empty house. He swore it wouldn't be empty long. They were going to be a family here. But first, he needed to see Meredith.

"How about we ask Mrs. Frank to let us move in right away? After, I'll show you the school where I almost failed first grade."

And where I first met Sydney Marshall, pretty as a picture in blonde pigtails. With big eyes, long skinny arms and legs, he'd been a goner from the moment he set eyes on her.

"You didn't almost fail first grade," Isabel scoffed.

"I did. See, what happened was..."

~*~

Fifteen minutes away at a fast walk, Syd tugged on the sheet covering Meredith and scolded, "You should be in the hospital."

Not that it did her any good. The woman lying between the white sheets of her convalescent bed had always been a dynamic, robust, take-charge woman. The stroke hadn't changed that facet of her personality, but her new frailty scared Syd; acutely brought back memories and the long ago helpless anxiety that had been her constant companion as she'd stood by with her mother, neither of them able to do more than hold her father's hand as he got sicker and sicker.

"Don't you worry. I'll be fine." Meredith patted her arm, understanding burning in her tired eyes. "Besides, I don't like hospitals. They're sterile, humorless places, full of sick people."

"You had a stroke, Meredith. That should buy you at least a week in the hospital."

Syd glanced at Doc Tucker, who was taking the older woman's blood pressure. His white bushy brows shot upward over round wire-rimmed glasses. He cleared his throat to cover a chuckle.

"I'll do better in my own home, won't I, Doc." It wasn't a question. More an order to agree.

The Doc's eyes took on an amused twinkle. "Here's as good a place as any to get your strength back."

He pulled the buds of the stethoscope from his ears and removed the blood pressure cuff with a loud rip of velcro.

Meredith pushed herself to a sitting position. Keeping her eyes lowered to her lap, she plucked at the covers, then reached for Syd's hand. "I have a favor to ask."

A bad feeling twisted in the pit of Syd's stomach. In all the time she'd worked for Meredith, the older woman had never once ask for a favor in that pleading way.

She curled her fingers around Meredith's. "Whatever you want."

Meredith hesitated, glancing up through her lashes. Syd frowned. That wasn't at all a needy look. "Stay for two months. Just until I get better."

Syd backed up a step. "Not that."

Meredith huffed out a breath. "Please?"

"You know I would, if I didn't already have a plane ticket and a job waiting for me in New York."

"But *The Gazette* needs you. He needs you."

Doc stowed the stethoscope and cuff in his medical bag. "Now Meredith, don't get yourself all riled."

"I finished the Columbia River Hotel piece this morning. It's on your desk. That should be the last in the series–" Syd was suddenly very confused. "Who needs me? The new owner?"

"I gave my word I would work with him for a year. To make sure he gets a good start."

Nope. Rosewood was not where the magic was. Hadn't been for way too long. Out there was where she would find the spark that was missing from her heart.

Breathing in and out slowly to calm the churning in her stomach, she leaned in and adjusted the pillows at Meredith's back. "I'm sorry, I *can't.* I don't have a place to live anymore. I turned in my notice at Rose Village and the landlady's already rented my apartment."

"At least talk to him. They'll be here any minute for lunch."

Syd felt herself giving in. How could she turn her back on Meredith? But if she had a dollar for every time her mother and this woman had talked her into something that put off her dream of living in an exotic city like New York, where there was life and excitement, she would be rich enough to retire by now.

Like always, the entreaty in Meredith's blue eyes pulled at Syd's resolve. "I'm not going to change my mind."

"I'm only asking you to talk to him."

"Well. Okay." Syd shook her head in resignation. She had the backbone of a caterpillar.

Her mother, and Meredith's best friend, Mayor Lauren Marshall, stuck her head in the room. "Lunch is ready."

Meredith dropped her good leg over the edge of the bed. "Help me get dressed."

"I'll leave you girls to it, then." All persons of the female persuasion were 'girls' to old Doc Tucker. He donned the worn fedora he was never without. "Don't over do it. I'll send Lucy by to check on you after clinic's done."

Syd helped Meredith get dressed, then settled her at the head of the dining room table – a regal Queen.

Dressing and walking the short distance from her bedroom clearly took too much effort, but this wasn't the first run-in Syd had with the stubborn angle of the Queen's chin. And it wasn't likely to be the last. Nothing was going to keep the obstinate woman from receiving her guests.

The door bell rang softly through the house.

"I'll get it." Lauren hurried out of the room, and when the doorbell pealed again, shouted, "I'm coming."

"You never said who bought *The Gazette*." Syd placed a tureen of stew on the table close to Meredith.

The woman sat straighter, fluffed her grey hair with her

good hand. "That's probably him now."

"Him, who," Syd whispered impatiently, then at the sound of her mother's laughter, looked up. And stopped breathing.

Startlingly familiar eyes, the color of Pacific Northwest storm clouds narrowed on her. They moved swiftly over her face, then took a heated swipe down her suddenly flushed body.

A flick of his gaze dismissed her, and just as abruptly a distant mask dropped, leaving a stranger eyeing her.

Benjamin Quincy was the new owner of The Rosewood Gazette?

Her heart hammering, one hand reaching for the back of the nearest chair, Syd faced the man who had once filled her oh-so-perfect world. In high school they'd been inseparable. And she'd loved him with her whole heart.

Pressing her lips into a straight line, she notched her chin.

In the intervening years she'd gotten over Ben Quincy. Over them. End of story.

TWO

*S*chooling her expression to mirror the dismissal hovering in the room like a flat cover of cold rain clouds, Syd refused to drink in every detail about the man the boy had become. She was made of sterner stuff than that.

But who had that much willpower, when a rock-you-to-the-soles-of-your-feet gorgeous male ignored a girl as though nothing of importance had happened between the two of them? She snorted under her breath. She'd been a kid back then. What had she known about happily-ever-after?

Still, eleven years dropped away in the space of a single heartbeat. The angles of Ben's face were filled in with age and experience, though little else about him had changed.

Not the long, lean length of him, still too hot for words in a buttoned-down, crisp white shirt, sleeves rolled to his elbows; with jeans riding low, fitting snugly over narrow hips. Not the rugged bad boy looks that in high school had attracted any girl with a heartbeat.

Brown hair, the color of molasses, was shorter than she remembered; the squareness of his jaw harder. The power he'd had in abundance to make her stomach tumble in a slow, knee weakening plunge reached out to trip her.

She stood straighter, returning the disinterested look in his narrowed eyes. What did she expect from the man? Roses and sunshine?

Out of the corner of her eye, she saw her mother and the Queen exchange looks. Syd took a big mental step back. *Oh no you don't.*

The two women who'd had the most influence in her life, were up to no good. As usual. If she wasn't careful, she'd find herself right in the middle of one of their scheming plans. Again. And that was one road she definitely didn't want to travel.

She grabbed her backpack from the floor by the sideboard. "Gotta go."

"But Syd–" They said in unison.

"What?" She snickered at the startled looks on the two women's faces, but then rammed headlong into twin furrows tugging Ben's brows together.

Bending to place a kiss on Meredith's cheek, Syd sent her mother a speaking look. "I'll talk to *you* later."

Throwing her shoulders back, she faced Ben. "It's nice to see you again, Ben. You're looking well."

She could have bit her tongue. She wasn't a coward, but when his brows arched, instantly taking her back to the time she'd worked so hard to forget, she couldn't hang around waiting for him to dispassionately return her conversational lobby.

Heading for the door, she tossed recklessly over her shoulder, "I'm late for an appointment. Enjoy your lunch."

When she brushed by him, and got unfairly snared by the faint, earthy cologne she remembered so well...too well, a girl peeked out from behind him.

They will be here any minute for lunch, Meredith had said.

Syd mumbled an apology for almost trampling the child, then practically raced out of the house, not slowing until she'd barricaded herself in her car. Hyperventilating, with her heart pounding in her ears, she curled her fingers around the steering wheel, straightening her arms until her shoulder blades dug painfully into the cloth covered seat at her back.

She wasn't running. Okay, it looked like she was running, but the truth of the matter was she'd needed fresh air to cool her heated skin, and to sweep the confusion Ben's sudden appearance had called up.

A long time ago, she'd purged Benjamin Quincy from her heart and mind. She had a life. Had designed a future that would be full of surprises and adventure, as far from the sleepy town she'd lived all her life in as it was possible to get.

She turned the key in the ignition. The unexpected return of an old flame was not going to interfere with her plans. No matter what memories he brought with him.

But he had a child. A girl. Who wasn't hers.

~*~

A storm raged out of control in Ben's chest. A blustery Pacific Northwester with enough gale force wind to knock him off his feet. This storm had a name. Sydney Marshall.

He'd thought the passage of time had put a dim patina on his memories. Of them, the perfect couple, he'd believed back then. The whole world their playground. And after that, a life spent happily married, raising a family.

He'd been wrong about that. About her.

What he needed was a swift kick in the butt for allowing himself to be rattled by the woman and the sharp clarity of returning mental pictures attacking the firm foundations of the life he'd built since.

Okay, so that foundation wasn't as rock solid as he'd hoped it would be. But what did it matter if the world had slammed on its breaks, skidding to a stop the moment he laid eyes on Sydney? And who cared that for a tiny kernel of time he'd crashed against the best, and worst, time in his life?

She'd been a mistake. They'd been a mistake. Two high school kids crazy in love, who'd made unrealistic plans to spend the rest of their lives together. It was youthful naivete, and in the end didn't mean a thing. A not-so-fond memory. Nothing more.

Life happened.

Just because it'd burned him up, the way she'd so easily kicked him out of her life, as though he'd meant nothing to her, didn't have anything to do with what was in front of him now. Yes, he'd taken his devastated hurt on the college party circuit. And yes, he'd changed the course of his life forever. He didn't regret the outcome one single bit.

Reaching for Isabel, he gently pulled her from behind him. There was room for only one girl in his life. And one objective. Make a happy, stable home for them both far away from the fast paced city life that so far had done neither of them any good.

Ben ignored the heat stirring in his gut belying his mental acrobatics. His dream hadn't changed that much. It just revolved around a different girl.

What did Sydney Marshall have to do with the business he was about to sign final papers on? Had she married while he was away? Did he even give a damn?

Meredith waved a fragile hand at the chairs closest to her. "Have a seat. Lunch is ready. You'll have to forgive Sydney. She wasn't expecting–"

Ben arched his brows.

Meredith shrugged. "So this is Isabel?"

Changing the subject to avoid the elephant in the room? He would allow it. For now.

"Yes." He settled Isabel at the table while Lauren put food in front of them. Stew and roast beef sandwiches. The perfect food for confession, he decided. "Isabel, this is Meredith and Lauren, Sydney's mother."

His girl nodded shyly, but Ben was glad to see the spark of curiosity move aside the lost look in the blue-green of her eyes.

Confession didn't get served until after the meal was done and Lauren, with a speaking look at Meredith, asked Isabel to help her with the dishes.

When Isabel hesitated, he nudged her along. Once she'd disappeared, her thin arms full of precariously stacked plates, he turned to his new partner. Meredith's chin angled. The move reminded him of his daughter at her most stubborn.

"If you want to know if my stroke's going to effect our

arrangement, it's not. Doc says I'm going to be fine. But until I'm back on my feet, I've asked Sydney to show you the ropes."

"And she agreed?"

"No. Not yet."

Ben scowled. "Look, I don't need Sydney's help. In college I did some work for *The Chicago Maroon.* I appreciate your offer to partner for the first year, but given the circumstances, I think I can manage."

"Running a town paper isn't the same as writing for a college weekly," Meredith huffed, sinking tiredly against the back of her chair. Ben leaned toward her. She waved him off with one hand, the other laying limply in her lap. "I should have told you before you left Chicago."

"Told me what?"

"*The Gazette* has been financially...unstable for awhile. Not so much that I would consider it bankrupt, but an infusion of money is desperately needed if you're going to be successful. I would tackle it myself, except it'll be a hard and thankless job, and I'm too tired and set in my ways to institute the innovation the business needs."

The fatigue and faint disappointment in Meredith's eyes softened Ben. "Don't worry about it, okay? It'll all work out."

Meredith shifted tiredly. "I asked for Sydney's help because she's worked at *The Gazette* for years. She's done the research. Knows what it will take to make the paper viable again. You need her."

No, he didn't.

Caught off guard, not by the information that the paper

was on shaky ground, he already knew that from his investigations into buying the business – he'd gotten a good deal because of it – but by the disappointment ballooning in his chest at Sydney's refusal to take Meredith's place. Which was ridiculous. And crazy.

He drummed his fingers lightly on the table. "I heard she's leaving."

"For New York." And before he could ask. "She's got a job with that fancy magazine, *The Traveler.*"

So she was finally leaving; like his ex, chasing after a better life. A mistake, he'd learned the hard way, but to each her own.

When he'd made the deal with the woman watching him warily, he hadn't bothered to checked the paper's complete employee roster. The one asset he'd been interested in was Clare Marsh, whose inspired piece on the renewal of Mount Saint Helen had been the primary reason he'd paid attention when he'd learned *The Rosewood Gazette* was for sale.

Though the talented travel writer wasn't the only reason he'd decided to buy the paper, if he hadn't read her story and seen her stunning photographs at the same time that Diana and her new husband had followed her fashion job to Paris – leaving Isabel in his custody – the idea of returning to Rosewood would never have occurred to him.

"How about Clare Marsh? She's still under contract, right?"

"Sydney is Clare Marsh." Meredith released a pent up breath. "I'll understand if you want out of our deal. I won't pull any legal shenanigans to stop you."

Clare Marsh's travel pieces made the newspaper special in its small niche market. He could build on that; increase circulation.

As his dream of the perfect life for Isabel began to crumble, Ben wondered what he'd been thinking? All he wanted was a return to the idyllic days of his childhood. Was that too much to ask?

He should have realized there was no going back. Not even for the love of a lonely, heartbroken ten year old girl.

The next day, Syd let herself into the building that housed *The Rosewood Gazette.* Dark, popcorn clouds dumped sheets of cold rain, while she fought with her own sense of drowning.

She couldn't get trapped in Rosewood. Not again. But, she hated telling Meredith no. Getting stuck in a cold downpour was little enough penance to pay for even thinking the word.

"And what *was* that yesterday?" she muttered, reliving the spike of attraction slicing into her when she'd laid eyes on Ben for the first time in eleven years? She'd buried those misguided feelings long ago.

This morning, tired of fighting with herself, and worn out from no sleep, while having breakfast at Rose's Bakery, Meredith's call caught her at a weak moment. She would do what she could for her ex-boss in the little time she had left in Rosewood, but Ben was on his own.

"What could she possibly want with these old issues of the paper?" She dropped the bound volume with a thud onto the front desk.

When she'd sweetly suggested Ben could bring the heavy book to her, Meredith had made a tsking sound and ended the call. So instead of working on her packing, here she was dragging the dang thing up from the morgue.

The bell over the door tinkled. The girl she'd seen with Ben pushed her way in, glancing furtively over her shoulder. Pink laces of what might have been new tennis shoes before losing a fight with the rain and mud, left a dirty trail across the threshold.

"Your shoelaces are un–"

Too late. One minute the girl was working up a snarky comeback, if the scowl aimed at Syd was anything to go by. The next, she was sprawled on the floor, anchored by a lace that had gotten caught in the closing door.

Syd knelt beside her. "Are you okay?"

Embarrassment stained the kid's cheeks. "Yeah."

The bell pealed again. The shoelace popped free.

"Isabel, I thought I asked you to wait in the car." Ben abruptly crouched beside his daughter. "What happened?"

Syd eased back on her heels. "Her shoelace got stuck in the door."

His concern instantly turned into a father's teasing grin. "Anything broken Princess?"

"I'm a dork, Dad, not a baby."

His grin wavered. Sad shadows darkened the eyes Syd

had fought hard to forget, then quickly disappeared as he lent a hand to help his daughter to her feet.

Little girls could be too careless with their father's feelings. She'd been the same with her own father. Easing to her feet, Syd put distance between her and the old memories. She wouldn't look back. There was no point in it.

But then, she did. Couldn't stop herself as she sat at her desk, her gaze singing back to Ben. Yearnings she'd thought dead, came out of hiding. Protecting herself against the onslaught, she crossed her arms over her chest; leaned back in the chair.

Tugging free from the protective hand on her slight shoulder, Ben's daughter jerked off the offending shoe. Leaving behind a muddy print every other step, she hobbled to one of the two chairs clustered around a small table where Meredith had a the Scrabble board set up for customers waiting for assistance.

Rain glistened on Ben's dark hair and suit jacket. Syd's heart squeezed. Illogically, she wanted to brush the water droplets away. "Come out in the rain to have a look around?"

"Actually, I came to talk to you. Meredith said I would find you here."

Syd straightened. So that was what the request for back issues was about. "So you bought *The Gazette*. Does that mean you'll be living in Portland?"

Housing was scarce in Rosewood, a distant bedroom community to the larger city. And she would be coming back to visit her mother and Meredith. It would make her very happy not to run into Ben every time she did.

He shoved his hands into snug jeans pockets, looking as uncomfortable as she felt. "Meredith is selling her rental on First Avenue. I'm buying."

Naturally. Syd absently played with the pencil she'd left on the desk blotter. The big white, two story house sat on a ridge overlooking Rosewood. As kids – best friends long before they'd begun dating – she and Ben had spent a lot of time sitting on a nearby bench, talking about everything and anything under the sun as they looked out over the town.

"He's forcing me to move here." Shoe back on and laces neatly tied, Isabel jabbed Ben's arm with a pointed elbow as she swept unruly, thick blonde hair off her face and into a long pony tail imprisoned by a band she'd fished out of her raincoat pocket.

Syd suppressed a grin. Who wouldn't like this child?

Ben rolled his eyes in her direction. "Isabel, this is an old...friend of mine, Sydney Marshall. We attended high school together."

That's not all they did together back then. Surprised by the sudden appreciation darkening the grey of his eyes as they flicked over her, a flush warmed Syd's skin.

"I'll bet he was a complete geek in school."

"Not so much. No." Grateful for the distraction, she ignored the tangle in her stomach.

Ben slipped an arm around Isabel's shoulders. "Mind your manners."

Syd wondered which one of them he was chastising in

that deep, low rumble?

Isabel wrinkled her nose, dipped a slight shoulder toward the mess on the floor. "I'll clean that up."

She was outspoken, strong-willed, and exactly the kind of child Syd had always wanted. With Ben. Someday. Swallowing back unexpected, and incredibly unreasonable, disappointment, she jumped to her feet, thinking...who knew what. "There's paper towels in the restroom."

Isabel disappeared down the hall behind the desk. Ben spoke in a low tone calculated not to reach his daughter's ears. "I didn't expect to find you here."

When her gaze snapped to his, he was too close, too intense, saw too much. "And, I didn't expect you to go right out and make yourself a daughter. How old is she, Ben? Ten? Eleven?"

It'd taken him a nanosecond to move on. And though that was exactly what she'd told him to do, she felt the flush of anger clear to her toes.

"Isabel's ten."

Immediately, Syd regretted her hasty words. She deserved his disdain. What he'd done with his life after she'd called it quits was no concern of hers. "I'm sorry. That was uncalled for. She's adorable. What is it you wanted to talk about?"

His lips pressed into a thin line, but disdain was not what she found on his handsome face. Confusion maybe. Then curiosity as he crossed his arms across his chest, taking a belligerent stance.

Isabel chose that moment to return, holding a fistful of paper towels. "Mom says I'm high strung."

Mom? An unwanted image of a younger Ben as she'd last seen him, holding a crying woman against his chest flashed through Syd's mind. An engagement ring had winked in the sun.

Isabel's bright eyes dulled before dropping to her shoes. "She won't let me go to Paris with her."

Okay. It was time to go. Unfortunately Ben had her blocked in.

He slid a comforting hand on his daughter's head. "Why don't you take a look at the Scrabble board. Looks like there's a game in progress. I need to talk with Sydney for a moment."

Isabel shrugged off the comfort her father offered, wiped the floor before half-slouching in one of the chairs while she pushed letters around in the nearest rack.

A sudden case of nerves attacked Syd. *She* didn't want to talk to Ben. "It's an ongoing game. There are no set rules for the players. Anyone can pick one of the racks of tiles and play a word."

Babbling. She winced.

"You're aware of how much trouble the paper's in?" Stormy greys settled on her flushed face.

"It," Syd cleared her throat, "has been for awhile."

"I need your help. Just until Meredith gets better."

She grabbed her backpack from the floor by the desk. "I can't. My apartment's been rented out. I have a non-refundable, one-way plane ticket to New York. And a job that starts in two weeks."

She advanced on Ben with every intention of forcing the ridiculously tempting man out of her way. He didn't move.

"I get that." He tilted his strong chin toward Isabel, who was laying down a word, every movement a pale imitation of a happy child, and lowered his voice. "We moved here to give her a normal childhood. She deserves better than what she's had."

He pressed his lips into a thin line. He didn't like having to ask. Syd didn't like him asking. "Meredith needs you. I need Clare Marsh. For a month. Maybe two."

She glanced at Isabel. Syd knew what that look on the girl's face meant. She'd had her own share of loneliness to deal with after Ben left, and then when her father followed suit. "Not fair, Ben Quincy."

He nodded in agreement. "Life is rarely fair."

A country song erupted from Syd's backpack.

"I'm not postponing the job in New York. It's the best opportunity to come my way." Ignoring the panic rising in her chest, she fished the cell out of the front pouch. "Hello?"

"Ms. Marshall?"

"Yes."

"Jim Hurley's assistant, Apple Davenport here." Jim Hurley was her new boss at *The Traveler.* "I'm sorry, but Mr. Hurley wants me to convey his sincere apologies. The job he offered you is no longer available."

A chill drove Syd around Ben to the window overlooking the street. "I don't understand."

"He decided it would be better to offer the position to someone with more...international experience."

Her stomach twisted into a painful knot, threatening to erupt in an unpleasant manner. "But, he said the job was mine."

"I'm really sorry."

No you're not! Syd wanted to shout.

"Mr. Hurley has authorized me to send a month's wages in compensation. What address may I send the check to?"

Address? She had no address!

Disbelief robbed Syd of speech. After a long silence during which she couldn't think of a single thing that would convince the assistant to talk her boss into giving the job back, she gave Apple Davenport her mother's address.

"I want to talk to Mr. Hurley."

"Mr. Hurley has left on vacation."

"For god's sake," Syd bit off the words.

"I'm very sorry," Ms. Davenport repeated.

"Of course." Syd snapped her cell closed and faced Ben.

From the glimmer in his grey eyes, he'd listened in and filled in the gaps. What could she possibly say? *I'm such a loser, I lost my job before it even started? Excuse me while I go vomit?*

The same disconcerting sympathy he'd shown his daughter, mixed with a dash of smugness that he'd gotten what he wanted, brought Ben to her side. Before he could knuckle rub *her* head like he had in the old days, Syd advised, "Don't get any bright ideas."

If he followed though with the understanding turning the storm in his eyes turbulent and dark; if he touched her at all; folded her against his chest the way he used to, she would crumble, turning into one of those watering pots she detested. Not that she was thinking he would, of course; she'd tossed that privilege away long ago.

Cell still in hand, she grabbed the bound newspapers; shoved the heavy volume into his hands. "Meredith is waiting for this. Since I'm sure you'll be seeing her soon, you can deliver it."

Shifting her backpack higher onto one shoulder and stalking to the door, she spun around. "This is just a setback. Temporary. There are plenty of jobs out there. Finding a new one won't be any problem."

She pushed on the door and walked, back straight, chin angled in defiance, into a cold, blustering wind.

"Sydney. Wait."

But she didn't, pretending not to hear the sudden concern lacing his rugged tone, like the finest Bailey's floating at the bottom of a stout glass of sinful cream.

THREE

*S*he needed air. To breathe. And think.

Syd was halfway to her mother's house by the time she realized she'd left her car parked in front of *The Gazette*. She waved a distracted hand at nothing. Didn't matter.

Huffing out a snort at her distraction, she pushed up the hill that led to the comfort of her childhood home. Ben was so...so...irritating! The image of him she had stored in her mind did not do the man any justice.

He was harder, except when dealing with his daughter. More closed off. Apparently on a mission to settle in Rosewood. And he was sexier than the most decadent brownie sundae slathered in warm chocolate she'd ever eaten.

That was the problem. She'd blown her chance with him eleven years ago, thinking she was doing the right thing. Now that she was about to leave for a new life, he'd returned.

And he was more attractive...more tempting...than she remembered. For so long, even before she'd had to forget her dreams and stay in Rosewood, she'd wanted the excitement of an adventurous life. The magic was still out there, waiting, but that road most certainly did not lead back to Ben Quincy.

Are you nuts? her inner crazy-girl wanted to know.

Ignoring the nagging voice, Syd shook the damp mist from her shoulders, then let herself into her mother's house.

Rubbing her hair dry with a towel from the closet in the guest bathroom, she made calls while pacing from the kitchen to the family room.

Of course the two jobs she'd turned down in favor of *The Traveler* gig were filled. She hadn't expected them to still be open, but had to try. Wrestling with nerves Ben's unexpected return, and the call from Apple Davenport had stirred up, she brushed her fingers over her father's old recliner while listening to the recording on the other end of the line.

Crossing her fingers behind her back, she left a brief message. The soft snick of the front door announced her mother's return. "Syd. What a nice surprise. Did we have a dinner date tonight?"

"You're home early."

They spoke in unison. The rest flew out before Syd could stop the words. "I lost my job."

"Oh dear. I'm sorry to hear that. I know how much you wanted the position." Lauren hung her raincoat in the hall closet before settling into the recliner. "Does this mean you'll be staying in Rosewood? I can't say I'm disappointed."

"I have feelers out. I'll find another job," Syd repeated the litany. If she said it often enough.

"I'm sure you will. But what about your old position at *The Gazette*? I know Meredith–"

"–asked and I said no."

"Well, that was before, wasn't it? It would be a shame to let *The Gazette* go under. Not when you need a job anyway. And while you're looking for something else, at least you would have a paycheck."

Astute. Pragmatic. Busybody Mayor Lauren, looking out for her town. That was her mother. And while the elder Marshall too often stuck her still unadorned fingers in where they weren't wanted, Syd loved her only relative.

But work with Ben? Wasn't going to happen. "I won't be here long enough. I've got a plane to catch."

Her mother's expression turned calculating. An alarm clanged in Syd's head. That look meant the Mayor was orchestrating something Syd wasn't going to like.

"When do you have to give up your apartment?"

"As soon as I finish packing."

"You can stay here, if you want, while you're sorting this mess out. For a couple of weeks, anyway."

Syd frowned. "A couple of weeks?"

"I have news of my own." Her mother looked around the room, a sad glance she quickly overlaid with a smile. "I've sold the house. I have a month to move."

"Why are you selling the house?"

Lauren raised an elegant brow, then shrugged. "You're off to New York. Since the house is too big for one person, I've decided you're not the only one who can make changes."

Syd dropped onto the couch. Her mother looked elegant in black tunic and leggings. It was a new look, she realized, surprised. "Where are you going to live?"

A perfectly manicured hand waved in the general direction of the river that wrapped around the west side of town. "I bought a condo by Deer Park."

"When?"

Like most small towns, folks in Rosewood knew everyone else's business. But, somehow in her hurry to get out of town, Syd had missed something vitally important.

Her mom tilted her head, gracing her with an amused look. "I'll bet you could eat. Let's go to the Ranger Saloon. We can talk about this over dinner."

Or perhaps not, Syd thought as her mind strayed to Ben. A riot erupted in her stomach. Things were changing in her hometown. But then nothing stayed the same, did it? And, change was what she wanted, right?

~*~

Friday, after school let out, Ben found Sydney at the Rock and Gem Show being held at the Rosewood High School gymnasium. He needed Clare Marsh and her talent. That his ex-girlfriend was the travel writer was an inconvenience he could have lived without, but with Isabel to take care of, he wasn't about to back down. Somehow he had to find a way to change Sydney's mind.

What he'd told Meredith was true. He could figure out how to make the paper viable on his own. The problem was, he didn't have the desire to become a workaholic in the process. It would take too much precious time away from Isabel. She'd already lived that life with her mother. She deserved more from him.

When he'd taken papers to Meredith to sign that morning, Sydney's mother had been there. A little charm had garnered the vital information, the daughter would be working one of the booths at the annual show. Hence this little side trip. It gave him time with his little girl, and an opportunity to corner Sydney so he could once more press his case.

And there she was looking as innocently pretty as the day she'd told him, in no uncertain terms, to get lost. She was a stunning, attractive woman, but he had no business noticing. Being a full-time single dad with a brokenhearted daughter to raise, and a business to get back on its feet, was more than enough to fill his plate to overflowing.

Ben locked his jaw against the arousal and anger building together. She could help him. If they could get past their broken history.

Taking hold of Isabel's hand, he plowed a path through the crowd to her booth where a sign advertised a thunder egg hunt at the top of each hour. She glanced at them with a welcoming smile.

When she saw who her next patrons were, her expression turned guarded, then softened as her gaze shifted to his little girl. "Hi Isabel. How's it going?"

Isabel raised one shoulders, then let it drop. A silent thunk resounded in Ben's chest. He wanted his child to be happy, but this battle was all uphill.

Sydney didn't seem to notice. "Have you come to participate in the thunder egg hunt?"

Isabel shook her head. Then for the second time since rolling into town, curiosity lightened her melancholy mood. "Can I?"

"Sure. The next hunt is about to begin. Go see George," Sydney pointed to a tall, angular, middle-aged man in a flannel shirt, blue jeans and sturdy hiking boots. "He'll get you started."

With a caution that pulled at Ben's heart, Isabel looked to him for permission.

He waved her off. "Go. Have fun."

She wrinkled her nose at him, making his heart wobble, then slowly wondered over to join the kids gathering around George, leaving *him* to focus on the dubious task of changing Sydney Marshall's mind, a skill he'd never actually had any luck developing to its full capacity.

"Have you eaten? Can you take a break?" He'd noticed a refreshment stand in the corner on his way through the gymnasium.

She didn't look at him. "There's not enough volunteers today."

Isabel's future was so much more important than Sydney's discomfort. Or his. "This won't take long."

Still she hesitated, but let out a long breath as though about to confront the lion in his den. As she put a *be-right-back* tent on the table, Ben frowned at the insulting image. He wasn't that bad or unapproachable.

"Ten minutes is all I can spare."

Once in line at the concession stand, despite how badly he needed her cooperation, he wasn't sure how best to proceed. The gentle scent of vanilla he remembered she favored disconnected his good intentions.

"Did you ever get married?" The question shot out with the speed of a bullet. Not what he'd meant to say, but then he was gratified when her heated gaze snapped to his from the inspection she'd been giving her worn boots.

"It's none of your business, but no."

It would have been his business, if...but never mind that. She was right. Ben hoped his smile was apology enough. "It makes sense that you would."

She eyed him, a wary kitty who didn't want to be petted. "Why?"

His slow perusal took in the sexy fit of her jeans; the way her turtleneck sweater snuggled her neck where only a lover should have access; the hint of pink that tinted her high cheekbones once he completed his survey. Finally he lingered on her full lips and let the truth rumble quietly from his chest. "You're a beautiful woman."

Sculpted brows drew together in such blatant disbelief he almost laughed. Cautious as ever. Long fingered hands he remembered with fondness seeking out the contours of his body, got shoved into back jeans pockets. "You married."

It wasn't exactly an accusation. Okay, it was. "Yes."

"So where's the wife?"

"The dot-com company I started at the same time Diana and I got married lasted longer."

"What went wrong?"

What didn't go wrong?

He ordered three hotdogs and drinks, then led the way to an empty table where he could keep an eye on Isabel.

There was no point in tying up the truth with a pretty bow. "We weren't in love, and Diana wanted a career in fashion design. So after three years, she took Isabel and moved to Manhattan. A few years later, she met her current husband, a man with a lot of clout in the fashion industry. He gave her what she wanted."

Enough of his story. He hadn't run Sydney to ground to discus his own dysfunctional past. "How's the job hunt going?"

The curiosity keeping her guarded gaze on him faded. A remote mask slid in place. "Still looking."

Seeing her eyes dart to her booth – his time was running out – Ben got right to the point. "I took a look at the article and pictures you turned in on the Columbia River Hotel piece. They're good. Really good."

The tension left her shoulders. When she smiled, the whole room brightened. "Surprised?"

"No. Of course not." His skin warmed a few degrees. He took a long pull on his pop. "I'm going to change the format of *The Gazette.* Move your column from the back of the paper to the second page. Why Clare Marsh, by-the-way?"

She eased away from him, pressing her back into the chair.

Back in the day, when their whole future dangled in front of them, she'd become a master at keeping him at arm's length. Old frustrations returned with a vengeance. If it weren't for Isabel and the paper, he would gladly put her the blasted plane himself.

"Clare Marsh, to honor my father," she said in a remote voice.

Clarence Marshall – the ghost that hung between them.

Sydney chewed her lip, a habit of long standing that in his younger days always left him wanting to kiss away her nerves. That much hadn't changed.

Ben slashed the desire before he did something stupid. Still, she deserved to know. "He would be proud of you."

"Maybe."

He frowned at that. What was she talking about? The Mr. Marshall he remembered had always been proud of his daughter.

The momentary vulnerability left her shimmering eyes. "Page two sounds great, but it's not my column anymore."

"That can be remedied. We'll negotiate a new deal."

Sydney scooted her chair back. "I won't be around long enough to negotiate anything."

He raised a hand to stop her and hoped he hadn't pushed his luck too far. "When do you leave for New York?"

"In a week." The clear brown eyes that scoured him shouted, *I'm fine. I can do this* – whatever this was – *without your help.*

She was shutting him out. Again. Fine by him. Well, not so fine, but what the hell. He had bigger fish to get out of the frying pan.

"I'll take it. And pay double your usual salary if you'll spend the week showing me everything I need to know to pull *The Gazette* back into the black."

Startled by his fast maneuvering, the rejection of his offer that had been forming stalled. Lips he'd used all kinds of excuses to kiss when they were teenagers, parted, inspiration for that part of his anatomy that should have little memory of the few times in high school when they'd been more than a boy and girl hanging out together.

But the laugh was on him wasn't it? She didn't need him then, and she didn't need him now. "Think about it. Two weeks salary for one week's work. I'm sure you could use the money when you get to the Big Apple."

It was the best he could come up with. If she still said no, he would have to find a more potent argument.

Resisting the stir of attraction cutting sharply into his gut, Ben slammed his defenses into place. He hadn't been enough back then and he'd learned to live with that.

Besides, this wasn't about saving what they'd lost. It was about starting over. He and Isabel. One last time before his daughter took the highway to troubled teenager.

~*~

Syd dropped her gaze to her barely touched cola, remembering the other time Ben had asked her to reconsider a decision that would change everything. Her father had just been diagnosed with terminal cancer. The doctors had offered no hope, suggesting only that the end would be long and torturous.

Ben was about to sacrifice every dream they'd ever had together when the reality of it hit her. He was walking away from college; the high paying job he'd dreamed of and hoped would take them on the adventure of a lifetime; denying himself the opportunity to see the world before they started a family.

Because of her, he was going to give it all up. Go work in his father's lumber yard, the one thing he hated and talked endlessly about *not* doing before her father's illness.

Knowing what she had to do, she'd cried for days before finding the courage to break it off with him. She couldn't be his ball and chain. She wouldn't be the girl who'd ruined his life, the one who kept him from pursuing his happiness. So, she'd sent him away in the most brutal way, making him believe she'd never loved him.

A lie told for a good reason.

By the time her father had convinced her to go after Ben, repair the damage she'd done to both their lives, it was too late.

She hadn't planned on staying in Rosewood as long as she did. It'd just happened; one thing leading to another. Now Ben was asking for one week. One week to help him while he made a home for his little girl in the town she was desperate to leave.

A resounding *no!* trembled on her lips, but how could she deny him?

Isabel rushed over brandishing a rock the size of Syd's palm. It'd been split open to reveal a milky white, crystal-like center. "Look what I found."

The child was practically dancing. Ben played along admirably. He bent close. "What is it?"

"A thunder egg. George said, since I found it, I can keep it. Can I, Dad? Please?"

He grinned crookedly. Syd froze.

"Looks like you're the proud new owner of a very cool rock."

Isabel returned his smile, the natural guardedness that touched Syd in a way she wasn't expecting, disappeared.

A spike of anger attacked her. How was it a mother did not want this precious child with her every second of every day?

"Can we go to the library and get a book on thunder eggs?" Isabel could barely stand still, and suddenly Syd wished *she* was the one allowed to take the child to the library.

"Sure."

That soft, gooey look he used to bestow upon *her* vanished when Ben's eyes lifted, all business now. His offer. He wanted an answer.

Before she could tell him, what? That she didn't need two weeks of wages? Was she crazy?

Isabel sobered, her slight shoulders slumping. "I wish Mom could see it."

Before she could stop herself, Syd butted in, "Maybe you can take a picture of you holding the thunder egg, and send it to her."

Syd slapped a hand across her mouth, but the hope chasing away the gloom that accompanied Isabel like a well worn shroud made the interference more than worthwhile.

"Can we, Dad?"

Ben's scowl wasn't encouraging. Syd refused to let him see her squirm. "I don't see why not. Your mom would like that."

With perfect timing, her cell vibrated. She checked the number calling. Thank goodness one of the messages she'd left produced results. Crossing invisible fingers, Syd turned her back on Ben and his pixie daughter.

"Hey, Tom." *Jacobson.* One of her college buddies. He'd been quicker off the mark than she; had defected to New York shortly after graduation, but they'd stayed in touch.

"Sorry I didn't get back to you sooner. I was in the middle of a cover shoot in Brooklyn." In the background a party was going strong. "Can't help you, girl. Wish I could, but I don't know of any jobs coming open."

Her shoulders stiffened with the effort it took to keep them from sinking in disappointment. "Thanks for checking. If you hear of anything?"

"I'll definitely call."

She snapped the cell closed; turned to face Ben. Both Quincys watched her, the father's expression thoughtful, the child's surprisingly curious. Getting drawn into their lives wasn't a smart idea.

At a small stirring behind Ben, Syd mentally backed away. Dressed for her Mayor's roll, black knee-length skirt and jacket over a starched-white blouse, her mother made a beeline for them, lips pressed into a firm, straight line. Never a *good* sign.

When she reached them, Lauren grabbed Syd's hand. "I

need to talk to you. Both of you. Over there."

She dragged Syd to the nearest corner away from the milling crowd. Ben naturally followed, despite the frown she aimed in his direction telling him to go away. Isabel sat at the table, tucking into the hotdog her father had gotten her.

Syd pulled free from her mother's grip. "What's going on?"

"The fund for the new library has been embezzled."

"All of it?" Her mother's nod was an angry jerk of her chin. Syd's stomach sank. "Who would do such a thing?"

"I don't know, but I intend to find out."

Despite the disastrous news, she was acutely aware of Ben's gaze on her face. "Have you reported the theft to the police?"

"Not yet. I wanted to talk to you first."

Ben's shoulder brushed against hers, the sting of excitement emanating from the contact a reminder that once there had been more than friendship between them. She concentrated on her mother's problem. "What is it you want us to do?"

"Information control. When this breaks, I want you to report it. An article in *The Gazette* that gives the facts, nothing more. And then any new information that comes to light."

"We can do that." Ben's dark brow arched. "Sydney?"

She played her last card. "I'm not a new journalist, I'm a travel writer."

Ben gave her absolutely zip for wiggle room. "You do

know how to write copy."

She released a resigned sigh. Her ex wanted one week. It looked like she was going to give it to him.

FOUR

*B*en leaned close to her mother. Maybe for the first time since he'd come back, Syd actually *saw* him. She'd been so busy working to prove how well she'd done without him, she hadn't looked past the boy she used to know.

The man he'd become was a stranger. Mahogany-colored hair cut above the ears, but still rakishly long enough to curl around his collar, was haphazardly tussled, as though a breeze had enjoyed fingering through it, the way her fingers suddenly itched to. A day's growth of whiskers lay heavy on his sharply chiseled face. Intriguing grey eyes periodically darted to Isabel, softening, while at the same time remaining fiercely protective.

This was a man of experience, not a boy untried by what life would ultimately throw at him. Confidence sat on his strong shoulders. A giddy feeling had her thinking he wouldn't bend easily to anyone's will but his own.

So what had happened to him while he'd been gone, besides marrying, having a baby, starting a business, divorcing, and taking on the role of single dad?

At that moment he caught her eye and winked in the same distracting way he had when they were teenagers and he'd caught her staring in class. Just like back then, she flushed, and a bit of the magic she'd been missing since her father's death challenged her to remember what it'd been like to be the sole recipient of Ben's attention.

Taken aback, she edged toward the booth she was supposed to be manning. It was no concern of hers what kind of man Benjamin Quincy had become.

Keeping an eye on her, he nodded at something her mother said before reaching out to stop her. "How about when you're finished here, we discuss the article for Lauren over dinner."

Syd tugged on her arm, not so much as to make a scene, but firmly enough to let him know she didn't appreciate being shackled. "Can't. Have things to do. Packing to finish."

A sudden glimmer from narrowed eyes made her stomach somersault. In a stupidly good way.

"At the office then. Tomorrow morning."

"Maybe." And when he wouldn't let go. "We'll see. If I have time. I'll try."

He dropped her hand then. Retreating to her booth with as much dignity as possible – after all she wasn't running from the stubborn man – she turned her attention completely to the folks who had questions. When the dust settled, Ben, Isabel, and her mother were gone.

Sighing, whether in relief or because she couldn't believe she was getting embroiled in yet another Rosewood drama, Syd kept herself busy. A few hours later she closed the booth and headed home.

Letting herself in the front door, she flipped on lights as she went, the faint echo of her shoes on the entry floor reminding her this cozy little apartment on the second level of Rose Village wasn't home anymore. She had a mid-town New York address. At least for a month anyway. Soon that would be her home.

Eerily silent, the apartment had a forlorn air, as half-packed places tended to accumulate. The posters she'd collected over the years of places she dreamed of seeing still lined the walls. They would be the very last things to be packed.

"Ship now, or after I have the new job?" she muttered, her voice sounding hollow in the half-packed room.

Turn right or left? She didn't know, so to take her mind off the surprising events of the day, off the images of Ben that hovered close, she turned on music, then went to cook up a cup of tea.

She'd never meant to be twenty-nine and alone. She'd dated some over the years with high hopes, but had yet to meet a man who could light her world like her dad had for her mom.

Only Ben had been able to do that.

She ignored the internal tic toc of her clock.

Yes, she fixed single cups of tea, but she didn't have to fight for the remote control, and on nights like tonight, a bowl of cereal, while hardly appealing, did the trick.

The rest of the evening would be simple. She'd spend some time on the internet checking out job boards, pack what she wouldn't need to use in the next week, and stop thinking about the man who had no place in the life she'd designed for her future. A good plan for an upwardly mobile lady on the verge of stepping into a bright adventure.

The doorbell chimed as the teapot stuttered into a whistle. Turning off the stove, she checked the peephole before flinging open the door. "What are you doing here?"

"Delivering pizza. And extra hands to help with packing." After a long moment in which she tried to figure out what Ben was really doing on her doorstep, his brows shot up. "The pizza's getting cold. Can we come in?"

Isabel shifted out from behind her dad, trying to see into the apartment. "I voted for Chinese, but Dad said you like pizza, and that his vote counted more."

The child was incorrigible. Syd reluctantly stepped aside. "I like both equally well."

He lifted the large box in his hands slightly. "On the table?"

"Yes." She closed the door behind them. Suddenly, her cozy apartment got a whole lot smaller.

Isabel's gaze darted immediately to the posters decorating the walls. When her feet followed her eyes, Syd faced Ben over the box he opened, releasing the spicy smell of warm pepperoni and cheese so it filled the room. "What's going on?"

"I figured you wouldn't have much food here. We were hungry, and I remembered you liked Papa's pizza." He stuffed his hands in his pockets, an endearing habit she remembered from before, when he was unsure of himself. "Meredith said you have some good ideas for improving things at *The*

Gazette. I didn't want to wait until tomorrow to review your notes."

This was awkward for him too, she realized. Stalling, she put plates and napkins on the table by the pizza. "Notes?"

He watched her move about the kitchen, his steady regard revving a different kind of hunger. "You always keep notes."

His gaze roamed over her face. Was he looking for the girl she used to be? If he was, that trusting girl was long gone.

Unwanted awareness churned in the pit of her stomach alongside an ache so surprising, and so profound, she forced herself to remember how completely it'd broken her when she'd found out Ben hadn't the same gut wrenching need as she'd had for him, even though her words at the time had said something else.

She'd accepted her own duplicity in their breakup a long time ago. There was no reason to go strolling down the yellow brick road now.

"I have notes," she finally agreed.

Placing a slice of pizza on a plate, she carried it to Isabel, who was staring at the Paris poster of the Eiffel Tower as if it held all the secrets in the world.

Ben followed. "You're leaving in a week. That doesn't give us much time."

Syd quietly panicked. *Time for what?*

Bumping the girl's arm gently with her elbow, Syd paid no attention to the father. "Isabel. Food."

Isabel took the plate, her eyes roaming from poster to

poster. "They're so cool. Have you been to all these places?"

"I haven't been to any."

Brows crowded together. "Why do you have them then?"

Glancing at Ben, Syd caught his startled comprehension. Suddenly normal breathing became impossible. It was no secret. "As long as I can remember, I've always dreamed of traveling to exotic places." *With Ben.* "Until I can, the posters are a reminder never to forget."

Lifting her chin, she turned a blind eye to Ben's speculation. Just because she wouldn't be traveling with him like they'd planned, didn't mean she'd forgotten.

Isabel whispered wistfully. "I wish I could go."

"You will someday," Syd encouraged.

"I want to be a model."

"Oh. Well, you'd make a..." Ben's quick, in-drawn breath warned her she was on shaky ground, but it was too late. "...lovely model."

Isabel lowered her eyes. Her lip trembled. Her plate tilted and the slice of pizza slide sideways. Syd steadied the child's hand, preventing the impending disaster about to happen on the carpet.

"I'm too clumsy. I don't walk with a glide." Isabel's voice quivered in misery.

Suddenly, for no good reason, Syd was angry. Ben had gone off and lived their life. Had their child. With another woman. And that child had been hurt.

"Who says so?"

"My mom."

Anger lacerating her heart, she looked from father to daughter. Isabel completely miserable. Ben looking like he felt completely useless, his hands curling into impotent fists.

This was absolutely none of her business. "Well. Then. There's something else you're probably good at doing."

"There is. She's—"

"Dad!" Isabel shot a speaking look at her father, frantically shaking her head.

Ben closed his mouth, the muscles of his jaw bulging with the force of his molars coming together. Isabel's desperate gaze bounced between Syd and her father. What quagmire had she tumbled into?

Growing an attachment for Ben's girl on the eve of flying off to another life was a very bad idea. Still she couldn't help sliding a comforting arm around the child's stiff shoulders.

"Don't worry about it. You don't have to be a model to explore all the exciting places in the world." Gently rubbing small circles on Isabel's back, Syd cleared her throat. "How about we eat this fabulous pizza you guys brought. Then we can pack. And when we're all done, you can pick out your favorite poster and take it home with you."

Sudden excitement danced in Isabel's eyes. "Really?"

"Really."

~*~

After a restless night's sleep, Ben carried a cup of coffee to a small table nestled in the alcove off Meredith's kitchen. Surrounded by windows looking out into a late blooming fall garden, he placed a pad and pencil on the painted blue surface beside the steaming cup.

Meredith had agreed to let them move into the house on First Avenue before the final papers were signed. The movers were scheduled to arrive next week. In the meantime, Meredith had insisted they stay at her place instead of the Fireside Inn where he'd originally booked a room.

Under the circumstances, he hadn't wanted to impose, but it'd agitated the older woman more when he'd stood firm, so he'd backed off and let Meredith have her way.

Leaning his forehead into his hands, Ben scrubbed his eyes with the pads of his palms. If he'd gotten more than a few hours of sleep last night, he'd be surprised. It'd taken longer than he planned to pack the rest of Sydney's apartment. They didn't get around to talking about what to do with *The Gazette*, so he'd managed to convince her to meet him at the office this morning.

How did women get so much...stuff...packed into such a tiny place? But that wasn't the real problem. The real problem had been dreams, one right after the other every time he closed his eyes, filled with images of Sydney Marshall. Sydney stretching to reach high cupboards. The occasional flash of a grin at something Isabel said. Organizing the work with relish, a devoted general to her cause as she gave orders to her troops.

She'd studiously ignored him in favor of a lopsided – on her part – conversation with his daughter. Standoffish in the beginning, Sydney had warmed up considerably to Isabel before the packing was done.

Isabel never took to strangers, but with his ex-high school flame she'd become a regular chatty-Cathy. And Sydney had been careful with her, as though she sensed how fragile his girl was. Even given their disastrous past, how could he not have the hots for the woman after that?

When he dropped his hands, Isabel stood in front of him, yawning, bed-hair wild around her sweet face, her sleepy eyes watching him steadily.

"Hey, kiddo. Want some breakfast?"

She dropped into the chair opposite him; folded arms on the table and laid her head down. "Yes."

He ruffled her hair on the way by. "Eggs and toast?"

She yawned again. "Cereal."

An easy search produced the necessary ingredients for a simple breakfast. He put it all in front of Isabel.

"Why is Sydney moving to New York?"

Ben sat across from her and swallowed a gulp of cold coffee. The kid could have asked an easier question. "Well...she's wanted to go there for a long time."

"Did you used to be boyfriend and girlfriend?"

He'd picked up the pencil, but it slipped from his fingers, clattering to the table. He stalled. "What do you mean?"

"Did you date?"

Holly cow. Arching his brows, he pinned Isabel with a firm look. "What do you know about dating?"

She shrugged in her too adult way. "I'm not stupid, Dad. I know a lot about it. Mom and Mike dated tons before they got married."

Ten was too young to know about these things, wasn't it?

"First off, I don't think you're stupid. And, yes. We dated." They'd had sex a few times, too, but he wasn't going to tell Isabel that. And after spending the evening with Sydney, followed by dreams that made sleep impossible, he had a feeling that youthful experience wouldn't hold a candle to being with her in that way now.

Retrieving the pencil, he reminded himself she was everything he didn't want in a woman. She made totally illogical decisions without talking to the man she'd professed to love, and without thinking through how those decisions would effect those intimately involved in her life.

She was restless. Reckless. Still searching for...he didn't know what. And she was stubborn, unbending, and after what she'd done back then, couldn't possibly understand the power of love and how together they could have conquered all their problems.

"You didn't marry her."

"No. Your mom and I had you instead."

"I like her. A lot."

So do I. "I have to go into the office for a few hours. Will you be okay here with Meredith?"

The doctor would be by soon. He and his nurse came every morning before clinic. Usually Meredith didn't make an appearance until after their arrival.

Isabel's spoon stopped midway to her mouth. Milk slopped into the bowl. "I want to go with you."

"There won't be much for you to do there. I'll come back

when I'm done and we'll go to the library."

"Will Sydney be there?"

He nodded. "We have some business to discuss."

"I want to go." She resumed eating. Apparently she thought that was the end of their discussion.

Frustrated amusement lightened his fatigue. He toyed with his coffee cup. He shouldn't think that was cute, right?

Ben sobered. Sydney was leaving, and it would be a train wreck if his daughter got too attached. It was his responsibility to set the proper example.

He and Sydney had a professional relationship. He was the boss, she the employee. He would see her at *The Gazette* and that was all. No more sending Isabel mixed messages by taking pizza to an old girlfriend. For the remaining week, that was completely doable.

"Okay. Finish your cereal and go get dressed." He glanced at his watch. "We need to leave in about thirty minutes. Can you get ready that fast?"

Isabel shoveled the last of the cereal into her mouth. Instead of answering, she carried her bowl to the sink and with a barely discernible skip, disappeared down the hall that led to their rooms.

Ben shook his head. This had disaster written all over it.

~*~

Syd sat at the reception desk, turned on the computer, and pulled up the report she'd put together for Meredith. It detailed her recommendations for modernizing the paper.

Chugging coffee to stave off the fatigue left from

spending a night reminding herself that handsome, charismatic, perfect-dad Benjamin Quincy did not have a place in her life, she printed the list, then scowled at the screen.

Still in possession of her key, she'd arrived early enough to do a job search. No luck. There were lots of freelance travel writer jobs, but nothing with a major glossy magazine, which would eventually – if all went well – provide her own column, and a steady income with benefits.

The bell tinkled. The door opened on a clear, sunny day almost as nice as summer. Ben ambled in, Isabel right behind. Rosewood was becoming too interesting, and too crowded.

Dressed in jeans and a soft, blue shirt, sleeves rolled to his elbows, he was regrettably the best looking guy in town, maybe even the whole state.

"Monday, we'll register you for school," he was saying.

"Do we have to?"

He spared Isabel a don't-mess-with-your-old-man look. "Yes. We do."

Isabel humphed, then spun, her hair flying around her face. She marched over to Syd. "Is that your red car out there?"

She smiled at the kid's attitude, and at the strained patience on Ben's face. "That's Stella."

"You named your car?"

Isabel's round eyes, accompanied by that disbelieving tone was so dramatic, Syd laughed. "Yup."

The girl turned to her father. "Dad?"

Grey eyes took on a stomach twisting twinkle, locking on Syd as he smothered a grin. "Not until you're eighteen."

"Darn!" Isabel tossed her head and escaped to the Scrabble board.

"Sorry we're late. We had a which-outfit-am-I-going-to-be-allowed-out-of-the-house-in crisis."

Syd glanced at Isabel. Looked like a black, heavy tunic sweater and matching leggings shoved into biker boots had won.

"Cute."

"She's going through a Goth phase. This was the best I could talk her into. Very scary before that."

Syd shoved the report she'd printed at Ben. "Here's my...notes."

Her cell rang. She dug it out of her pocket, noticed the number and frowned. "Mom, what's–"

Lauren's words were rushed. Syd covered her mouth. "Oh, God."

She flipped the phone closed, grabbed her backpack and headed for the door.

"What's wrong?" Ben reached out to stop her, but she adroitly avoided his hand.

"Meredith fell. She won't let the ambulance take her to the hospital."

Ben and Isabel ran after her. "We were just there."

Syd had no response to make that would dislodge the lump in her throat. Jumping into her car, she sped toward Meredith's.

FIVE

"*Of* course I'll stay with you." Syd squeezed Meredith's hand. The older woman's eyes were closed. Fatigue marked her face.

Doc Tucker finished his exam and stuffed his stethoscope in his bag. He waved the emergency folks off who were filling out forms at the end of the bed. His gaze collided with Syd's over Meredith.

"She's going to need round the clock assistance for the next few days. If we can't get someone to stay with her, I can have a room ready for her on the convalescent wing of the May Woods House by this evening," he said evenly.

"I'm not going there."

Syd kissed Meredith's forehead. "It's only for a few days. They'll be able to keep an eye on you. Make sure you don't fall again."

Meredith opened her eyes. "You can stay with me." The tired blue orbs pleaded with her. "You have to get out of your apartment anyway. Where will you go if not here?"

"To Mom's."

"She's in the middle of moving. Stay here. Ben will help you."

Stay in the same house with Ben Quincy? Not an ideal solution.

"Please?"

Syd couldn't fight the woman who'd helped her through the toughest time in her life. Hating it, but accepting the inevitable, she relented. "I'll get my things while you take a nap."

"I'm not a child. I don't need a nap."

At that moment her aging mentor sounded just like Isabel.

"Well, you're going to take one, or I'm going to hire Nurse Ratchet to come stay with you."

"Alright," Meredith grumbled, letting Syd slide the covers to her chin. "I'll take a nap. But only because you ask so nicely." Her eyes started to close. "You'd better be here when I wake up."

Syd smiled as Meredith drifted off, then sobered. She could stay until it was time to catch her plane. Surely by then, there would be no need for her to hang around.

Ben motioned her over from the doorway; leaned close. "I'll stay with her while you take care of whatever you need to do."

His close proximity, the brush of his breath as he murmured the words, the note in his deep voice that said he cared about Meredith as much as she did, sent a shiver skipping down her spine, of ill-timed regret that she'd broke it off with him all those years ago.

Her reasons had been sound. And there was no going back now.

"Are you sure?" She could have bit her tongue off at the

inane question. Of course he was sure. The Ben she remember wouldn't have offered otherwise.

He lifted a sheaf of papers in his hand. She saw it was her report on *The Gazette.* "I have some light reading to keep me occupied."

"What about Isabel?"

"She's watching a movie."

But Isabel wasn't in the family room. She hovered behind her father, a line of worry beginning to form between her delicate brows. "Is she going to be alright?"

Syd brushed by Ben, ignoring the scent of his shaving lotion and the way it made her want something she couldn't have. "Meredith is going to be fine."

"Where are you going?"

"To finish packing the apartment."

Isabel's lips trembled. A tear slid from the corner of one eye. "Can I come with you?"

Syd's barely cobbled together composure crumpled some more. It would be so easy to love Ben's girl. "Sure, if it's okay with your dad."

She glanced at Ben. Given their history she would understand if he didn't want his daughter hanging with her, even for the short time it would take to close the apartment. But she couldn't abandon his little girl either, not if she was reading the panic flooding Isabel's innocent eyes right. It was the same dread clamoring for a foothold in her own chest, that once again she might have to watch someone she loved fight desperately for their life.

Her heart stopped its beat when he hesitated a fraction too long before saying, "Alright."

Isabel scooted around Syd to give him a sloppy kiss on the cheek. Her heart almost resumed its normal rhythm, a little too excited by the man looking at her as though wondering if he'd misplaced his trust.

Picking up his challenge, something long buried kicked in her chest. She would make sure he hadn't.

"Thanks, Dad."

His wary gaze never faltering, Ben slid his arms protectively around Isabel, "Be good."

"I will. I promise."

I promise, too. I won't disappoint you. I won't let your little girl get hurt.

~*~

Several hours later, Syd had packed her travel bags, taken down her posters with Isabel's help, and arranged storage for her furniture and boxes at Rosewood Self Storage on the edge of town.

By putting everything there, she wasn't admitting her bid to begin a new life in New York had hit the skids. Only that it was smart to wait and send for her belongings when she had a job that would last longer than a week.

The whole time, she answered Isabel's unceasing questions. About Rosewood. Growing up in Rosewood. Going to school in Rosewood.

She wrapped her hands around her caramel macchiato. They'd finished off the day at Darla's Coffee Clutch, a quaint little place decorated in country-style secondhand furnishings, where Isabel continued her interrogation with, why was Sydney leaving Rosewood?

"Well, I've wanted to take pictures since I was in high school. And I figure New York would be a good place to take them." She shook her head. That didn't begin to describe what drove her. What part of her dream would a child understand? "I'm looking for magic."

"What kind of magic?"

Syd wasn't sure herself. "The kind that makes everyday sparkle with excitement."

"How will you find it?"

"I don't know. I guess I just keep looking until I do."

"How come it didn't work out between you and my dad? Didn't you like him?"

Syd nearly spewed out her drink. *Like him?* That was the understatement of the year, but she wasn't going to go *there*. Not with his precocious ten year old. "My dad got ill. And your dad went off to college. We didn't see each other after that."

It wasn't a complete fabrication. She wished the devastating months that followed had been that simple. She swallowed more coffee past the lump in her throat and changed the subject. "So you start school on Monday?"

Isabel's shoulders dropped. "Yes."

Syd lowered her cup to the table. "Aren't you excited?"

"No."

"Why not?"

"I don't make friends."

"I find that hard to believe."

"It's true. I'm smarter than the other kids. They don't like it."

"Smarter? What do you mean?"

Isabel laid her forehead on the table. It muffled her voice. "Math and science are easy. Like playing a game."

Syd suddenly understood. "You're that kind of smart." A prodigy.

"I guess."

"Isabel, that's wonderful." Frowning at the wretched hiccup coming from the child, she wavered. "Isn't it?"

Isabel looked up, her eyes dark with heartbreaking unhappiness. She whispered brokenly, "No. It's not. Nobody likes me. I never have any friends. Mom says it's because I'm too smart and I should try harder to act dumb."

Appalled, Syd sat back in her chair. What mother would think her child was 'too smart', then lay the burden of the lack of friends or social skills on that child's fragile shoulders, without helping her find her way in the academic world of kids, who were often brutal to those who were different?

Isabel straightened. "*You* could date my dad."

The abrupt left turn surprised Syd into blurting, "I can't."

"Why not? We could do things together."

And suddenly is was very clear what was behind Isabel's bold invitation. The child wasn't asking a woman she hardly knew to go out with her dad. She was asking that woman to include the man's daughter in their dates. She was looking for a full-time mom.

But Syd didn't have a clue how to be a mom to this precious child. A chill skipped down her spine. She didn't want to be the one to tell Ben's little girl that dating her father was not part of the program.

~ * ~

When the front door opened and closed with a sharp snick, Ben looked up from the notes he was studying. Isabel marched passed him to her room. It took a moment for him to recognize the look on his daughter's face. A long moment when his thoughts stayed tangled with Sydney's notes. Her suggestions for restructuring the paper, and then doing an on-line version were brilliant. Combined with his own ideas, they could do something special with the periodical.

One of the first things he needed to do was see his banker. Relaunching *The Rosewood Gazette* was going to take some capital.

The door snapped closed again. Syd carried bags of groceries into the kitchen, her expression as closed and forbidding as his daughter's.

Frowning, he put the papers aside and went to help her, pulling a gallon of milk out of one of the bags she'd put on the counter. "You girls have fun?"

"Yes."

The word was clipped, demanding he back off, which of course made him want to know more. "Do you need help unloading the car?"

"No."

He took a bag of bagels from her. "What's wrong. Did Isabel misbehave?"

She grabbed the bagels back; tossed them on the counter. "No, she didn't misbehave. She's a good kid."

Ben watched as Sydney struggled desperately to reign her temper in, and failed. "I'm baffled is all."

So was he. "What do you mean?"

"It's none of my business."

Irritation getting the better hand, Ben stopped on his way to put apples in a bowl on the counter. "But, what?"

Sydney snatched the fruit from his hands. "How did Meredith do while I was gone?"

"She was still sleeping the last time I checked, which was about ten minutes ago." He shoved his hands in his pockets to keep from throttling the woman who was taking over too many of his thoughts. "Just spit it out, Sydney."

She spun to face him. "Alright. Your daughter has some concerns."

"What concerns?"

She seemed at a loss for words. "She...she misses her mother."

Ben went very still. "I know she does, but Diana lives in Paris now."

"Well, Isabel wants a woman in her...your life."

He narrowed his eyes on the lady who could bring out his ire faster than it took to get stung by a bee when messing with their hive. "*What* did she say to you?"

She stared at him.

There could only be one explanation for her cranky anger. He took a wild stab. "Did she ask you to be that woman?"

"Like I said, it's none of my business." Sydney dropped her heated gaze, and busied herself with emptying the second bag.

If she wanted him to feel like an ass, she'd succeeded. A cocoon of silence, as his mind struggled with what she wasn't saying, settled heavily on his shoulders.

What had her response been? All of a sudden he was aware it was just the two of them in the kitchen. Not like the old days, but something new and unexpected. Here was a woman who cared that his daughter was feeling the separation from her mother in a way only another girl could understand. And it bothered her. Brought out her mama bear. Made her cross the invisible line she'd drawn between them the first time he'd seen her upon returning to Rosewood.

Despite their history, Ben, for no good reason, itched to close in on Sydney. Test the waters. Find out if sparks would fly when he kissed those pursed lips. Stupidly his pulse leaped eagerly.

He scratched the day old beard he hadn't taken off that morning, noticing how ringlets of hair fell around her delicate face. The conversation had started out being about Isabel needs. How had the turned into one about his?

"Don't worry about Isabel," he told the woman putting invisible roadblocks between them. "I'll take care of my daughter."

Her hands filled with fresh vegetables, she notched her chin. "You do that."

"I will," he promised in soft warning.

Before he could follow through and brush the wayward wisps of sunbeam hair off her cheek, Ben spun, heading in search of his daughter. He found her stretched across the bed, her fingers pulling at the ruffled pillow sham.

"So your outing with Sydney didn't go well, huh?"

"Don't be such a putz, Dad. I had fun," she murmured forlornly into the bed covers without looking at him.

"Putz, huh? Have you been watching old movies again?" he teased, sitting on the side of the bed. He covered her shoulder with his hand, the only love he was capable of at the moment swelled into a warm cushy cloud that engulfed him with one purpose. "You know you're the most important girl in my life, right?"

She shrugged under his hand, but still didn't look at him. "Sure."

With one clear thought, Sydney Marshall was relegated to the rear of the train, somewhere behind his daughter. There was no such thing as a magic pill to make things all better. It would take hard work to create a good life for Isabel in Rosewood. Hard work he was more than willing to do. So it didn't matter that he was stirred up over an old girlfriend. Protecting his daughter from getting hurt, no matter what the cost, was the first – and only – thing currently on his agenda.

When it suited Sydney – in five days to be exact – she would get on that plane and do what she did best. She would sever their ties, however thin they might be, and leave him and Isabel dangling in a cold wind.

Ben locked his jaw. Good thing this time what was left of his world wouldn't be so frigid. He had his little girl. Her birth had saved him at a time when his life had been in pieces. It was time he returned the favor.

He draped an arm around her shoulder. "How about a trip to the library? We can get those books on rocks you wanted to check out."

Isabel nodded; dragged herself off the bed and curled into his chest. Her enthusiasm was a little feeble, but he would take what he could get. "Alright then, let's go."

~ * ~

Syd waited until the door closed behind Ben and Isabel before coming out of the kitchen. Why had he chosen a woman who, from all appearances, didn't want to be a mom, when she, Sydney would have made an excellent mother?

Yes, yes, yes, she'd been the one to send him away. For good reasons, she still believed. She'd tried to make it right, but then capricious fate had taken charge, and she'd been too late to fix her mistake.

So feeling like Ben had left her out of the most important part of his life was childish. She tossed the towel she'd been using on the counter. The best thing she could do was have nothing to do with Benjamin Quincy, or his dynamite little girl. But somehow she was already hip deep in the muck with him. At the paper. Sharing Meredith's home.

To stay the thoughts swirling in her head, she went to check on the other woman, and found her reading, glasses perched on her pert nose.

"You're awake."

Meredith set the book aside. "Haven't been for long. Did I hear Ben and Isabel?"

"You did, but they left. Are you ready for a bathroom break?"

Swinging her legs over the side of the bed, Meredith waved her off. "I can do this part."

Syd ignored her, offered an arm, which Meredith took hold of with a snort. "What do you want for dinner?"

"Something light and easy."

Easy to Syd meant microwave popcorn. "How about soup and a sandwich."

"That would be fine." They shuffled to the adjoining bathroom. "I want to get dressed."

Syd helped with the dressing part. In a short while she had Meredith settled in the living room with a tray on her lap, steaming soup and a turkey club waiting to be eaten. Her favorite blueberry tea was at her elbow.

All the while Syd wondered where Ben and Isabel had disappeared to. Not that they had to report in to her every time they left the house.

"Your mother stopped by earlier. Seems the Council has figured out who embezzled the library fund."

The Rosewood library had flooded twice in heavy rains

over the last few years. The town council was fund-raising to get seed money for a building on higher ground. "Who was it?"

"Darcy Burke."

"The Finance Director's assistant?"

"She's gone to Cancun on her honeymoon, so there's been no formal charges yet."

Stunned, Syd settled in a chair near Meredith, balancing a tray on her lap. "I went to high school with Darcy. She was so shy. It's hard to believe she would do something so...illegal."

"There's good and bad in everyone. Won't know the truth until she gets back," Meredith shrugged, tasted her soup before leaving the spoon in the bowl, then leaning back in her chair. "Ben's a good father, don't you think?"

It took Syd a moment to catch up. Lust. Want. The sister emotions twisted like sirens in the pit of her stomach at the mention of his name. But not need. Never need.

Silently she agreed with Meredith's astute assessment. Her ex-boss' thoughtful gaze stayed on her, but Syd wasn't interested in talking about Ben.

Naturally that didn't stop the other woman from poking around. "Looks like some of the old flame might still be there. On his part. And yours."

Syd's cheeks warmed. "I'm not interested in resurrecting old flames."

"I've seen how you look at him, young lady."

And how is that? She groaned. "Nothing going on there."

"You sure?"

Stung that there could be some validity to Meredith's observation, she cast an unyielding glance at the woman sitting comfortably a few feet away. "When my dad had so little time left, I made a mistake and squandered precious moments chasing after a fantasy that had no basis in reality. I won't do that again, Meredith. Not for Ben Quincy. And not for a silly attraction that has no basis in reality."

"You don't think your *silly attraction* is real?"

Syd remembered the last conversation she'd had with her dad. The promise she'd made to settle for nothing less than an extraordinary life.

Promise me you'll find a man who loves you the way I love your mother.

She'd thought that man was Ben, so she left her father to fight for that extraordinary life, and instead had gotten a crushing, rude awakening. When she got home, it was all finished but the crying.

Guilt she thought had eased over the years washed over her. She whispered. "No. They're not."

"What if you're wrong? If memory serves me right, Ben was as hot headed as you. Hot blood and a broken heart are not a good combination for anyone."

Syd pressed her lips together. "I'm not wrong."

Ignoring the pitying look in Meredith's eyes, she carried her unfinished lunch to the kitchen, back ramrod straight, dignity taking the high road.

SIX

It was easy to avoid Ben for the rest of the weekend. He took Isabel into Portland to see the sights, and by the time Monday morning rolled around, Syd had had enough of herself.

She rose early and immediately got to work submitting her portfolio and resume to the Human Resources Departments at five big, glossy magazines. There were no openings, but someone had to see her work and decide she was a must have.

When Ben and Isabel joined her and Meredith at the breakfast table, she had her emotions – and her attraction to Ben – well in hand.

"So what are you two doing today," she inquired with just the right amount of casual interest to prove she'd recovered complete objectivity.

"We're going to register Isabel for school, then I'm going to *The Gazette* to get acquainted with the layout there. We can meet back here at noon, if that's okay with you."

She told herself to appreciated Ben's brisk, professional attitude, and tried not to snort her coffee through her nose. What she had in mind would be a whole lot easier if she wasn't constantly ogling the way firm muscles filled out his starched blue shirt. "While you're gone, I'll work from Meredith's office."

The doorbell chimed. Seconds later, her mother was pouring coffee. She refilled Syd's cup before sitting across from Isabel. "Don't you look all grown up."

When Isabel smiled shyly and scooted her chair back to carry her breakfast bowl to the sink, Syd got a good look at what the kid was wearing. A black, long sleeve tee-shirt, two sizes too big, with the faces of a popular heavy metal band covering the entire front, black stovepipe pants, and heavy soled black boots. Her hair hung in her face. Lip gloss gleamed on her lips.

Syd's brows rose in surprise. Ben's snapped together.

Isabel, hands twisting together, turned pleading eyes on Syd. "Will you come to the school with us?"

Before she could find a good reason why she couldn't, Ben made her excuses. "Sydney is staying with Meredith today."

A tiny dash of disappointment pinched somewhere near Syd's heart. Which was crazy. No way did she want to accompany the newest citizens of Rosewood on what amounted to their first family errand in their new hometown.

"I don't need a babysitter," Meredith muttered. "I fell because that darn cat insisted on wrapping himself around my ankles."

Larry. Meredith had coaxed the animal into the house when he was a feral kitten. Syd shot the older woman a stern look. "We'll see what Doc says."

Isabel's shoulders slumped.

Too aware of Ben and his daughter, she felt her own

shoulders begin to sag. Her mother's quiet tones interrupted the awkward silence. "I'll sit with Meredith until Doc gets here. Take as long as you want. I don't have anything important to do until this afternoon."

Out of the corner of her eye, Syd caught the wink Lauren sent to Meredith. They often did that when they conspired together. The universe in the form of one ten year old child and two conniving women was definitely not on her side.

Isabel's face lit like a Christmas tree. "So you'll come with us?"

Syd didn't want to get embroiled in their lives. Glancing at Ben, she wondered how to politely say no, when his girl wanted her to go so badly?

Isabel's pleading look, and Ben's frown tipped the scales. What could it hurt to help the child get over being nervousness because she was starting at a new school? A little insanity never hurt anyone.

She pasted a big smile on her face. "Sure. Absolutely. Would love to."

Lauren and Meredith smiled smugly at each other, dang it.

Isabel clapped her hands in delight.

For a second, Ben looked harried. On a rough sigh, he pushed a hand through his dark hair. But when he looked at her, the mask was back, covering his thoughts.

~*~

In the main office of the Rosewood Middle School, Ben registered Isabel as memories of a skinny, fearless girl with corkscrew blonde curls assaulted him. How in the heck had he gotten out of the house with Sydney Marshall playing a supporting roll to his Mr. Dad?

Getting her help with *The Gazette* while she was still in town was one thing. Giving her entry into his private life was something else all together. It should be him and Isa, not you-and-me-and-kid-make-three. But the pleading look his daughter had given Sydney, and the way she'd jump in to help, despite the fact that she hadn't wanted to – she never could hide her feelings – had made any objection he might have raised obsolete.

The woman had not lost a bit of her spirit, which was sexy as hell, damn it.

Isabel pulled on his shirt and whispered. "Dad, don't tell them about you-know-what."

He handed the woman on the other side of the counter, a Mrs. Carpenter she'd told them, the packet of transfer papers Diana had given him from Isabel's last school.

He leaned close to whisper back, "You can't keep it a secret. You're a year ahead in school. They're going to figure out why."

Blue-green eyes the same shade as her mother's widened in panic. "I don't want anyone to know."

Ben met Sydney's quizzical look over Isabel's head. Here they were again, so many years later, in the Registrar's office. Only this time they weren't getting a firm dressing down for running in the halls. The hint of vanilla he'd always loved, mingled with smells of food being prepared in the cafeteria."I can wait outside." The low, husky sound of her voice, as if she remembered too, pushed everything but the kiss he suddenly wanted to indulge in – and shouldn't be thinking about – from his mind.

"No! I want you to stay." Isabel grabbed Sydney's hand.

Ben didn't need Sydney seeing how inadequate a father he could be, but because his baby seemed to need her, he silently implored her to stay.

To his surprise, Sydney, didn't go from zero to sixty in thirty seconds in the judgmental department. She let Isabel lean into her without flinching or sending him an exasperated look. That was all it took to kick his inconvenient attraction for the woman into overdrive.

Unexpectedly she knelt to Isabel's level. "There's nothing to be worried about here. Your dad and I both went to this school. You'll like it."

"Promise?" Isabel's lip quivered. Ben's chest hurt, and just like that he wanted to do the most unforgivable thing. Hug his daughter...and the woman kneeling so close to her...in public, something Isabel had already, many times forbidden him to do.

"Promise." Sydney agreed solemnly, hooking him like a starving fish who'd just swallowed a juicy worm with the hook.

Can't happen, Quincy. Don't go there.

Mrs. Carpenter shifted through the papers he'd given her. "According to these records, you're very advanced in math."

Isabel closed her eyes and sighed heavily. "Yes, ma'am."

"I'm going to have you talk to one of the counselors, Ms. Penhollow. She'll set up your schedule and get you in the right classes."

When they entered Ms. Penhollow's office, a middle-aged, petite blonde, with curious puppy-dog brown eyes, rose to greet them. "Syd, today's not your day to tutor, is it?"

"No. I have a new friend who's here to register."

Ben tried to be casual about the spark that ridiculously poked him in the chest. "You teach here."

Sydney blushed. Her clear topaz gaze locked with his. "I tutor kids who are behind in their reading. Wednesday is my last day."

The woman was incredible. When he'd first come back to town, he hadn't expected her to still be in Rosewood. But she was, and her life seemed so full. Why then, did she want to leave?

Brutally severing the cord drawing him inexplicably to her, Ben turned his attention back to Ms. Penhollow. She was smiling at Isabel. "This must be our new student."

Not liking how easy it would be for Sydney to become part of who he and Isabel were together, he stuck his hand out to the counselor. "I'm Ben Quincy. This is my daughter, Isabel."

Jenny, according to the tent sign on her desk, was the perfect distraction. Dressed neatly in slacks and light sweater, her office had that well used look. Sticky notes, papers and books were piled on every available surface.

Ben appreciated that she didn't make a big production

out of the fact that somehow he'd fathered a genius, who wasn't happy with the fact that her skill with numbers made her more brilliant, and therefore different, from most of the other humans on the planet.

When Isabel haltingly admitted she wanted to learn to play the sax, he was drowned by the need to kick something solid as his father-of-the-year rating slipped another notch. How had he not known that?

Jenny signed Isabel up for band, then printed her schedule.

"I'll show you where the lunchroom is, but will have to leave you there. I have a meeting that's about to start." She glanced at the institutional clock on the wall. "It's been nice meeting both of you. A student will be along shortly to show Isabel to her home room."

They followed Jenny across the crowded common area to the lunchroom, where she left them to wait for the promised escort. Isabel sat at one of the tables and immediately commenced drumming her fingers. He settled beside her, while Sydney took the bench on the other side.

Letting his gaze roam over Sydney's familiar face, emotions sputtered he didn't dare name. She was exceptional with Isabel. Though she'd tried to keep her distance, her soft heart went out to his daughter anyway.

Tension eased from his shoulders. Any outsider looking on would swear she was the mother instead of Diana. But she wasn't Isabel's mother, and never would be. Not in the ways that counted most.

Hastily he turned the page on his uneasy thoughts. "The place hasn't changed much, has it."

"New paint job last year."

She's as nervous as Isabel. Surprised, he leaned on the table toward her. Why? He nudged Isabel's shoulder. "Sounds like we need to buy you a saxophone."

Isabel drew circles on the table. "Mom would never let me take band."

"At Christmastime, the school band and choir perform all over Portland." Sydney cut off the words when a boy swaggered into the lunchroom, heading in their direction. Her lips compressed into a thin line. Ben had to agree with her.

He stopped in front of Isabel. Dressed entirely in black, matching hair was slicked to the side. A heavy metal chain hung from his front pocket.

Ben was looking at the poster child for a kid heading down the wrong path.

"You Isabel Quincy?"

"Yes." Isabel's eyes went round. She straightened in her seat.

Out of the corner of his eye, Ben saw Sydney frown. He groaned and laid a restraining hand on his daughter's shoulder.

"I'm Kevin Newman. Ms. Penhollow sent me. I'm supposed to take you to your home room." The boy hitched his head toward a hall leading away from the lunchroom. "Come on. You don't want to be late." *Not that it matters,* his bored tone implied.

"See ya, dad." Too eagerly in Ben's opinion, Isabel grabbed her backpack and hurried after Kevin.

"I'll pick you up after school," he called to her retreating back, raising his voice in the hopes she was listening.

She was smarter than the average kid. Maybe he shouldn't send her to a co-ed public school after all. Maybe one of those all-girl brainiac schools would be better.

He watched until he couldn't see her anymore.

"She'll be okay."

Sydney had leaned across the table. Her long, tapered fingers squeezed his arm. The warm understanding in the eyes that collided with his went straight to his gut; did not pass go; did not collect any reward.

A wave of something that was more than lust overran him.

"I need strong coffee. Now."

~*~

Ben swallowed a burning gulp before he took a good look around the place Sydney had brought him to. Rose's Bakery took up the first floor of a small, prettily painted Victorian house. The floors were wooden and not exactly level. A glass case of baked goods greeted customers when they walked in.

Tables of varying sizes occupied the rest of the space which was loosely divided into three rooms. And the smell. The sweet aroma of warm pastries was enough to make any bachelor drool.

Sydney, the prettiest girl he knew – even when she was his eight year old best friend – watched him over the rim of her cup, one of those vanilla, non-fat something-or-others. A pudgy apple fritter dripping in glistening sugary topping sat neglected in front of her.

"She'll be okay."

"I know." He sighed heavily. "When Kevin came into the lunch room, a funny look crossed your face. Anything I should know?" *Since my daughter has taken an unreasonably short time to decide she liked the boy, same as I did when you came into my world.*

Sydney carefully put her coffee down. "He's one of the kids I've been tutoring."

She paused, obviously trying to choose her words with care.

"You may as well tell me." He locked his jaw. Isabel was everything to him. "I intend to find out all about the kid anyway."

She leaned on her elbows, chin in hand. "Kevin doesn't have the best home life. His father's an abusive alcoholic, and while his mother does her best to protect him, most of the time he's the one doing the protecting."

"Why doesn't the state take him out of there? Or the mother leave the bastard?"

"The state has tried, but Kevin runs away and goes back. He has a little brother." As if that said it all, Syd shrugged a slender shoulder. "As to why Jillian doesn't leave? Why does any woman stay in that situation?"

Ben leaned back. Families like Kevin's were everywhere, large city or small town. Still it was a harsh reality he hadn't expected to find in Rosewood. "Is there anyway we can help him?"

Sydney's concerned gaze bored into his. In the light brown depths caution swirled. It set him back a step to realize she didn't trust him. That shoe should be on his foot.

"I always thought if Kevin could get a good job–" She left the rest unsaid. He noticed she had a habit of doing that, something that was new.

But he would mull that over later, because all of a sudden he wanted to prove she *could* trust him. If she would let herself. "So, like I said, your ideas for *The Gazette* are interesting."

Out of nowhere, a possessive arm dropped around Sydney's shoulder. A sudden spike of anger slammed into Ben's gut as he narrowed his eyes on the stranger who'd taken a seat next to her as though he had the right to be that familiar. "Hey Baby. Gran said you were here. How's Meredith today?"

The simmer turned to a boil. She had a guy?

Both his girls.

He stopped right there. What was he thinking – *his girls?* And what was he, sixteen again? Sydney Marshall wasn't his girl. Those days were long gone, like water under the proverbial bridge.

"I'm Grant Reed, Syd's, er...friend."

A friend with privileges from the look on Reed's face as he pulled Sydney close.

Ben took the offered hand, squeezed harder than he

probably should have. "Ben Quincy."

Steely eyes sized him up. "You staying in town long?"

"Bought *The Gazette.*" His temper careening out of control, Ben tossed enough money on the table to cover the tab, then scraped his chair back, before letting his gaze slip to Sydney, noting she hadn't moved from beneath Reed's arm. "Thanks for going to the school this morning. It meant a lot to Isabel."

He stalked out the door.

Unfortunately it'd meant a lot to him too, but he kept that firmly to himself.

SEVEN

"What was that all about?" Syd demanded in a whisper.

Grant removed his arm from around her shoulders, the sappy grin on his face that had her brows snapping together, disappearing. "An intervention. You looked like you could use one."

"Thanks. I think."

All she knew was there was a moment – when she could see the wheels turning in Ben's head – that he was considering giving a troubled teenage boy a job at *The Gazette*, and she'd gotten the bum's rush from a sudden urge to throw her arms around his neck and kiss him silly.

"Something wrong with your Apple Fritter?"

She pushed the plate away. "I'm not as hungry as I thought."

He slid the plate toward him and broke off a large piece. "What are you going to do if you don't find a job?"

She made circles on the table with her fingers, thinking of Ben's retreating back, how stiff his shoulders had been. Had he known she'd, for the count of a single second, forgotten she was the one who'd sent him away and why? That she'd suddenly wondered if the spark could be re-lit between them, and flamed into something better than they'd had before?

"I don't know."

"You can come back to work here. Sleep on my couch if you want."

Eleven years ago she'd started coming into Rose's to drown her grief and guilt in fattening pastries and lattes. Over the next month she'd spilled her sad story, gained ten pounds, and because she was in everyday, Grant had talked her into putting her time at Roses's to good use working the second shift around her job at the paper. They'd been the best of friends ever since.

"Why didn't we ever get together? You know, date or something," she surprised them both by asking.

Grant's brows arched. "Or something?"

Embarrassment flushed her face. "You know what I mean."

Grant laughed. "Do you want to go out? I have a friend at The Nines in Portland, who could save us a good table."

Syd shuddered. "Heck no."

"That's why we never went out. You don't like me that way. And while you're a terrific best friend, I can't see the two of us ever achieving liftoff together. No disrespect intended."

"Liftoff?" Syd sputtered, then laughed until her sides hurt. Amusement lit Grant's clean-cut face. Wiping the moisture from her eyes, she assured him. "None taken."

Scooting her chair back, she pushed the money Ben had left toward Grant. "I've got to get back to Meredith, but thanks for helping me put things in their proper perspective."

"No problem. Come by anytime. My couch is always available. In a non-sexual way, of course."

Grinning, she waved good-bye, got into her Volkswagen, and sat there for a long time. There were four days left until she got on the plane to New York. Grant's question was valid. What if she *didn't* find a job by then?

She could still get on the plane. There was no reason not to. She'd paid first month's rent with a hefty deposit on an apartment situated on the Upper West Side. She had a little cushion in her bank account to get a ticket back if she needed one.

Crossing her fingers, she whispered a little prayer she wouldn't have to use it. And wished her momentary lapse back in the bakery hadn't happened. What she'd briefly felt was bigger, more startling than the intense innocent feelings she'd had for Ben in high school. Her heart thumped hard.

Turning the key, she ordered her fickle organ to be quiet. The engine come alive with a grumble. Syd pointed the car toward Meredith's. The ride was brief, but long enough to consider that time was running short, and there were still some things she *had* to get done.

As she parked the little Bug in front of Meredith's house, she smiled at Grant's so-called intervention. Only a good guy would be willing to step between a friend and a runaway train.

A great guy.

Ben's serious face popped into her mind, but she ignored the nudge, instead grateful for Grant's quick thinking. He would make some woman a great husband someday, as long as that woman didn't mind competing with his geeky love of online gaming.

She found her mother and Meredith sitting at the table, heads bent over a game of Scrabble. They looked expectantly at her when she stopped in the kitchen to put water in the electric teapot.

"So how was your morning with Ben?" Lauren inquired as if it was as natural as lambs being born in the spring for her to go with him to register his daughter for school.

She pressed the 'on' button with more force than was necessary. "It turns out Isabel's brilliant in math."

Meredith and her mother raised perfectly sculpted brows in unison. In fact both women were dressed in their best shopping cloths, their going-out makeup applied just so, not a strand of hair out of place.

"Ben certainly loves that girl, doesn't he? You can always tell a good man by how he treats children. I bet, on a date, he'd show a girl a good time." Meredith played her word on the board.

Syd gave them both a stern look. "Maybe *you* should ask him to go on a date?"

Meredith shot her a sassy grin. "Maybe I will."

Lauren's response was to lean toward Syd. "He's very good-looking."

"How about we talk about something else." *Something not so disconcertingly personal.* "What did Doc Tucker say when he came this morning?"

Meredith waved one hand negligently. "He said I'm doing better than he expected, didn't he, Lauren?"

Her mother nodded.

"And, when I told him you'd be available to stay for the rest of this week, he said he'd check with my insurance company to see if they will pay for in-home care."

One worry slid off Syd's shoulders. How could she, in all good conscience, have deserted Meredith if the older woman truly needed her? A sigh of relief had her leaning back in her chair. "That's good news. So, what's the plan for today?"

Lauren rose from the table. "I've got a meeting with the Clackamas County Sheriff. Then I'm coming back to get Meredith and take her to a quilt show at the May Woods House."

Hence the fancy clothes and elegant faces.

On her way to the door, Lauren handed Syd a folder. "Here's the initial notes for the article on the embezzlement. We don't have any solid proof of who did it, so you can't name names, just write a brief front page article."

"Can do."

Her mother kissed her temple. "I know you can, sweetie."

Syd glared in sudden suspicion at the file clutched in her hand. "Shouldn't you give this to Ben?"

Lauren winked at her. "You won't mind doing that for me, will you?"

Keeping her exposure to Benjamin Quincy to a minimum would be a better idea. "No, of course not."

"I think I'll read for awhile."

Syd helped Meredith stand. The vague sound of the front door opening reached her, followed more clearly by a familiar masculine voice mixing with Lauren's. A shiver of expectation trickled down her spine as some not very nice words escaped under her breath.

When Ben entered the room, she blurted, "I thought you were going to *The Gazette.*"

Heat transferred to her face warming her skin. Too untamed to stop there, it skimmed down her neck, then her spine, dang it.

"I did, but I couldn't get past security on the computers. When I got a call from the moving company, I decided to come here and work. They're ahead of schedule. The truck will be at the house this afternoon."

Meredith swayed. Syd pushed back the attraction making her witless, and reached out to steady the older woman. "Let me help you."

The feelings pounding her had to be lust. She'd gotten over wanting more of Ben Quincy a decade ago.

Meredith pushed her hand away. "I'm fine. Doc said so. You two go on. The next issue of *The Gazette* comes out next week. I'm sure you have a lot of work to do."

Plucking a book off the counter, Meredith slanted Syd a pregnant look, then shuffled carefully into the den. Syd turned on Ben. She'd managed to make a life without him. She didn't need the considering gaze taking a quick, sizzling swipe from her eyes to her toes. And she wasn't about to start wishing things had turned out different between them.

Her pulse bounced anyway. She moistened suddenly dry lips. Pressed a hand to her belly. "I should have mentioned the passwords on the computer. With everything, it slipped my mind."

He shrugged, his stormy eyes settling on her lips. A shiver composed of mostly unbridled want tripped along her spine.

Whirling into action, Syd scooted by Ben, careful not to brush him on the way. Grabbing her laptop from the bedroom she was using, she opened it on the breakfast table, her back to the man and the tension that had suddenly sprung between them. "If you want to use the computer in Meredith's office, I can work from here. I have remote access."

Fortunately he heard the back-off warning in her attempt to put some physical distance between them. They worked semi-companionably for the rest of the morning and into early afternoon, but the aware tension hovered, no matter how much Syd was determined to make it go away.

The good part was she remained close enough to assist when Meredith needed it, but truthfully, the ex-newspaper woman wasn't stretching the truth when she'd insisted she felt better. Over soup and sandwiches, the three of them argued the pros and cons of moving to a web press versus staying with the ancient, but still working, sheet fed press housed in the basement of *The Gazette.*

It warmed Syd to see Meredith's feistiness return, but not as much as the quick banter Ben tossed her way. Before they were through for the day, they'd thoroughly dissected the benefits – or not – of having an online version of the paper, in addition to the newsprint version.

It was like old times. And the biggest surprise of all was

discovering she liked being in on the planning process; liked rebuilding a newspaper from the ground up. Having a say was fun, and she was impressed that Ben listened to her ideas, rather than relegating her to the role of travel writer who contributed her polished piece and nothing more.

The way he carefully listened to her advice, tested the soundness of her recommendations, gave her confidence. Another surprise. But not enough to cross over the canyon she'd dug between them. Despite the approval brimming in the eyes that frequently settled on her face, he didn't want her on his side of the divide either.

She turned off her computer. It was time to call it a day, before she got tangled in Ben's glossy web. Again. And this time she had more to lose than her first love. Who she was, and her future was on the line.

First it had been her father, then Ben, who'd picked her up when she fell and scraped her knees. After her father's death it was her mother and Meredith. She had to find out if *she* was capable of rescuing herself when she got knocked off her feet. Now was the last chance she was going to get.

Closing the laptop, she turned away from the refuge Ben offered, and disappeared into her temporary room.

~*~

Ben gathered his papers, his mind whirling with the business plan they'd come up with, but not whirling half as much, or with as much electrified energy as he had after discovering Sydney had a boyfriend, then spending the better part of the day while they worked together, irritated because of it.

He resisted the urge to follow her.

How serious could Sydney be? The guy never seemed to be around. He, on the other hand, found himself absurdly wanting to spend as much time with her as possible. Loads of time that had nothing to do with work.

He glowered at the papers in his hand. It was ridiculous how much he enjoyed seeing her lips lift in a smile, or that flash of amusement at some pushy remark Meredith made, and the tiny, sexy crinkles that flared out from the outer corners of her eyes when she outright laughed.

At the school earlier, she'd shown an incredible insight into Isabel's heart, the girl's own mother didn't possess. It knocked him off balance.

Stuffing the papers into his brief case with little care to protecting the pages, he agreed with the voice arguing for the opposition. Okay, yes, obviously she was deeply involved with folks in town. Kevin was a perfect example. She actually cared what happened to the chain-wearing kid. And damn it, because she did, he did, too. He hadn't felt this...engaged...in a very long time.

And yes, she'd changed in the years he'd been gone. For the better, his traitorous heart conceded. Wanting to disagree, he closed the briefcase with a sharp snap.

Meredith had told him how she'd stayed with her dad until the end. *More than once.* He thought about it for a moment. *More than twice.*

But sensing how amazing she'd become – she'd always

been amazing – for the first time since that long ago, life shattering day, something didn't ring true about the way she'd ended it between them.

At the time, hurt and angry, he'd honestly believed she'd used her father's illness as an excuse to push him out of her life. What if he was wrong?

Damn it! He gave up the fight and followed Sydney to her room. "I have to go get Isabel. Come with me."

The stubborn look she gave him actually had Ben smiling, until he saw the vulnerability lurking beneath it. A defenseless ache was there, then gone, and he wondered if he'd even seen it in the first place.

"I have an idea I want to run by you."

Her cheeks turned pink as if she could read his mind and was thinking she'd like to rumple the neatly made bed too. Edging around him, she stalked to the front of the house. "Don't you have a moving company to meet with after you pick up Isabel?"

He glanced at his watch. "We'll talk on the way."

"I have to stay with Meredith."

Ben raised a brow at her determined effort to avoid being alone with him. For the present, the excuse would have to hold, until there was the soft sound of the front door closing.

Meredith appeared in the doorway to the den, keeping her balance by hanging onto the wall. "You don't have to babysit me. There's your mom now. You kids go on. And don't come back early on my account. I'm going to talk Lauren into having dinner in Portland."

Joining them, Lauren chimed in, "Sounds like a good plan to me."

Ben didn't give Sydney a chance to come up with another excuse not to accompany him. "Great. Let's go. I don't want to be late. Isabel doesn't like that. She already thinks it's bad enough I've moved her to a town away from her friends. I don't want to find out what she would think of being left to wait on the front curb of the school by herself."

Sydney snickered, the sound going through Ben like a forgotten firecracker. A smile teased him from topaz eyes. An old ache he'd thought long gone found purchase in the pit of his stomach when she said softly, "Coward."

He headed for the front door. "You bet ya."

They were halfway to the school when he broke the silence that had gathered quickly between them. "I want to hire Clare Marsh to do a bi-monthly column."

She slid a guarded look in his direction. "You can't afford Clare Marsh, and besides–"

He cut in. "I know. You're moving to New York." He braked at the next corner to let a young mom pushing a stroller cross the street. "You're right. I can't pay full-time wages. But if we continue to use the old sheet fed press, that'll save the expense of a new printing machine for now. Then, I think we can negotiate a salary, or a per piece scale if that's what you'd rather."

He kept his expression friendly. Open. No tricks. No hidden agenda. At least that's what he told himself. "You can live anywhere. The only stipulation is that I want your column to focus on travel in the Pacific Northwest."

He parked in front of the grade school and turned in his seat to study Sydney. She stared at her interlocked fingers. The autumn sun caught on strands of moonbeam-colored hair spiraling along the sides of her delicately curved face. His pulse took an unexpected leap.

"I'll think about it," she finally said, so quietly he had to strain to hear.

That was better than he'd hoped to get. Pushing on the door handle of the vintage Camaro, he glanced at the kids milling at the front of the school, and stopped before getting the door fully open. Isabel stood on the lawn to one side of the entrance, her eyes locked on Kevin Newman.

"What the heck?"

"Looks like Isabel's making friends."

He grunted. "Is it time to unpack my gun and make a show out of cleaning it when the boys come over?"

"No. She's ten. That doesn't come until she's at least thirteen," Sydney laughed, the sound rushing through Ben like the tumble of a white-water river.

"When did your dad bring out his guns?"

Her laughter died away. Ben looked at her; realized he'd touched a raw nerve.

"I was twelve. It was my first dance. Billy Harrison was my date."

He couldn't help it. His lips twitched. "I remember that dance. He wore his basketball shoes with his Sunday best, tripped on the hem of your dress, and knocked you to the floor with his elbow. Whatever happened to good old Billy?"

In the deep shadows of her eyes he saw the struggle to restrain sudden amusement. Something inside him went soft.

"He's married, has three kids, and works as a welder at Gunderson in Portland."

Feeling like the world was tilting at a dangerous angle, he managed to withstand an insane urge to take one of her hands and intertwine his fingers with hers. He raised a questioning brow.

"They rebuild rail cars."

"That sounds like a dangerous occupation for a kid who had two left feet."

"You're not a nice man, you know that, right?"

"So I've been told," he agreed in droll seriousness.

Then he got his wish. Sydney laughed again, and the afternoon took on a gut warming brightness.

A knock on his window startled him out of his irrational preoccupation with the woman beside him. They'd been here, done this before, and it hadn't turned out good.

Pulling himself free, he rolled down the window.

"Dad, can I go to Rose's Bakery with Kevin?"

He shook his head. "We have to meet the movers at the house, and I want you there to tell them where to put your things."

A familiar mulish expression sprouted. "But, Dad–"

He thought quickly. Before she could get a full head of steam, he cut her off at the pass. "Ask him to come over. We can use the extra muscle."

The stubborn look vanished. "Thanks, Dad." With a grin, she ran back to the boy waiting, his hands shoved in his pockets, his face immobile.

"Good save, Dad," Sydney whispered as she leaned over to watch the two kids.

"Remind me of that later. We were never that young."

"We were younger." The soft words were laced with a longing that pulled at his gut.

He let his gaze travel over her face. In his eyes, she'd always been beautiful, but now there was more than beauty there. "I'm going to have to get used to this, aren't I?"

"Yes, I believe you are," she said wistfully.

Isabel came back, with Kevin following. Ben had yet to feel the heavy weight of being a parent as much as he did at that moment. From Chicago, he hadn't been able to influence his daughter's life in New York much. And because she'd spent her formative years under Diana's benign neglect, in her desire to be all grown up, Isabel had her feet firmly planted on the fast tract.

It had always been his job to worry about her, and protect her. He winced. So far he hadn't done a very good job of it.

As she scooted into the back seat, he narrowed his eyes on Kevin. The kid returned his stare. "Sir?" He was asking permission. Good boy.

"Come on, Kevin," Isabel said, her tone threaded with worry.

Ben capitulated. He couldn't seriously keep her locked in her room forever. Though he wanted to. He motioned with a jerk of his head. "Get in."

The tension in the boy's shoulders eased off. "Thanks," he mumbled in the direction of his shoes.

Hoping he wasn't doing the wrong thing, Ben started the Camaro. He wasn't sure of the sudden idea clamoring in his head.

Three hours later, household possessions crowded the open rooms of the first floor of his and Isabel's new home. Other than directing the movers about the placement of furniture and boxes, he'd kept quiet and listened as Sydney talked to both kids as though she wasn't leaving in four days time, and had all the time in the world for them. Their camaraderie reminded him of what he'd come to Rosewood to do.

Kevin started for the door, waiving negligently at Isabel as he passed her. "See you at school tomorrow."

Ben stopped him. "Heading out?"

"Gotta get home."

"Do your parents know you're here?"

"They don't care," Kevin shrugged as though it didn't matter, and when Ben waited, shuffled his feet. "I have to fix dinner for my kid brother."

"Can I talk to you for a minute?" Without waiting for the boy's response, Ben led the way to the front porch, at the last minute before the screen door closed behind him, catching Isabel's scared look. Twin furrows channeled between his daughter's brows. "I'll be right back."

In a straightforward manner Ben had to admire, Kevin

faced him, his shoulders square, ready for trouble. The boy was big for his age. Not as tall as Ben, who topped six foot, but someday he would be. His blue eyes were wary. Black hair chopped in uneven layers hung in disorder to his shoulders. He was lanky, and restless.

The breeze moving gently across the porch was balmy for a Northwest fall evening. A hint of danger filled the space between them, but only because Kevin was expecting the worst, Ben realized.

He glanced into the house. Sydney, one hand on Isabel's shoulder watched them. He tumbled into the startling depths of her eyes and nearly got lost in the shimmery depths.

Cutting himself free from the seductive woman, he cleared his throat and turned back to the boy. There was a lot at stake here. For Isabel.

Telling himself he wasn't doing this for Sydney, but for the business that would provide his daughter with a stable home, he told Kevin, "I want to hire you. If you're interested."

Guarded surprise splashed across the kid's face. Caution won out. Ben was glad to see it.

"What kind of job?"

"I'm going to need some help running presses at the newspaper. Think you can do that?"

Kevin shoved his hands in his pants pockets. "Sure."

"When do you turn thirteen?"

"In a couple of weeks." He notched his chin in defiance. "I was held back a year in school."

"We can look into getting a work permit, but it'll be

after-school, two days a week for now. And you have to keep up your grades. Do you still want the job?"

Kevin stretched to his full height. "Yes, sir."

When Ben ran into Sydney's soft smile across the threshold, his stomach fell several stories.

To Kevin, he said, "Okay, the job's yours."

EIGHT

The rest of the week passed mercifully quick. In order to keep her mind on tying up loose ends instead of on hunky Benjamin Quincy, Syd resorted to making an old fashioned list. Nowhere on the page was there any mention of getting involved with her super-sexy, hot ex-high school sweetheart and his daughter.

She wanted to keep it that way, but every time she turned around, there he was. Knowing eyes the color of a surprise clash of wind and rain, watching her. Yummy dimpled chin. Male body tall and as strong as an oak – life's vulgarities hadn't cut *him* off at the knees. He was a feast for any thirsty woman's eyes.

Syd tightened her itchy fingers on the pencil.

Find a grant benefiting small town newspapers – check.

She'd found a literacy grant that specifically helped small newspapers update and retool, so they could keep up with changing times. All Ben had to do was write the grant request.

Develop a promotional plan aimed at The Gazette's existing customer base. Target new customers – check . Nearly complete.

Reintroduce Ben to Rosewood's business community – working on it. After hours when her mother could be with

Meredith, who still seemed a bit wobbly.

Her thoughts shifted to Meredith and the request they'd made to her insurance company for in-home care. There was still no response. The last thing Meredith wanted was to go to a residential care facility. Syd didn't blame her. Her ex-boss had been independent all her life, running the paper on her own terms for more years than she could remember.

After her fiancé had run off with her sister, Meredith had made her life exactly what she wanted it to be. These were all stories Syd had grown up on. And she admired with everything she had in her the other woman's fortitude and strength.

She wanted to live by the same ideals and hoped that's what she was doing by moving to New York. Tapping a nail against the keyboard, her mind drifted right back to Ben, dang it, and the smile that lightened the grey of his eyes, when he looked at his daughter. She dragged her list closer.

Next week's edition was ready to go. A banner splashed across the front page announced the twice-monthly's new publisher. *The Gazette* had a new look; new everything.

She was pleased with how it'd turned out. Hopefully Ben was too. In fact, he and Kevin should be at the press right this minute getting ready for the job ahead.

She'd had her last tutoring session with the boy yesterday. He was so excited, he'd hardly been able to sit still, but she remembered Ben's instructions. His new employee had to pass all his classes to stay employed.

So she'd kept him at his reading lesson a little longer

than usual, the last chance she would have to impress upon him how important knowing how to read well was going to effect everything else he did in life.

The doorbell rang. She hurried to answer it before the chiming disturbed Meredith, who was taking her usual afternoon nap.

Kevin's agitated look greeted Syd, making her stomach roll. Was Ben hurt? "What's wrong. Was there an accident at *The Gazette*?"

"She's gone."

"Who's gone?"

"Isabel. She's run away."

"Why? Where did she go?"

"She said she was going to Paris. France?"

"Oh hell." Syd grabbed her bag. "Have you told Ben?"

"No. It's my fault. We had a fight." His Adams apple bobbed. "I thought... She likes you."

"Stay here with Meredith," she commanded, pulling out her cell and dialing the main number at the paper.

"I want to go with you."

She stopped him with a firm hand to his shoulder. "Someone has to stay with Meredith. Can you do that for me?"

With a shaky nod, he reluctantly agreed.

Syd grabbed a slip of paper from her bag. Cell lodged between ear and shoulder, she quickly wrote scribbled her number. "Meredith's napping right now, but if there's any trouble, call me."

She shoved the paper into Kevin's hand and ran to her

car.

~*~

Ben uncurled from under the press and arched his back to get the kinks out. The smell of dust, newly cleaned heavy machinery, and oil permeated the basement.

While exploring every crevice of the building in order to acquaint himself with his new business, he'd found an old, tattered instruction book on how to maintain and operate the ancient machine. It was in a drawer of an equally ancient bank of wooden cabinets that lined one wall of the press room.

So while Sydney worked from Meredith's on the details of putting the paper on the map, he'd been the master of avoidance, cleaning the press, surprisingly looking forward to the moment he would turn the thing on for the first time. Today was that day.

Despite the fact that Sydney had cleaned out her desk here, the stubborn woman's touch was everywhere. In the posters of exotic destinations on every available wall of the place. In the uneven stacks of books about the Pacific Northwest, sticky notes with her handwriting marking pages of interest. She used to do the same with her school books in high school.

Here he'd figured she'd moved on after her father's passing, and all this time she'd been snuggled in, carving out a nest for herself, though she didn't seem to know it. The girl he'd had an adolescent crush on – and that's all it had been – was a pale wraith, compared to this woman he'd discovered in her place.

His heartbeat clamored, anticipating her next call to discuss some obstacle she'd encountered, or the solution to a problem he'd thrown in her way just to see what she would do with the challenge. She was brilliant. Why she hadn't bought *The Gazette* herself was a mystery. She certainly knew more than he did, about what it would take to keep the business going.

They could make quite a team, publishing the newspaper together. For an insane instant, he wondered what it would be like, after all this time, to be more than teen sweethearts. How would it feel to hold her close, slip his fingers through the blonde corkscrews of her hair, and press her body to his?

Would the fireworks be the same? Or different. Better? Brighter? More stunningly magical for the time they'd been living separate lives?

He shook his head in dismay. *Forget it, Quincy. Not going to happen. Can't go back.*

No matter that she'd emerged from her cocoon a stunning butterfly, she was still the same girl who'd deliberately walked out on the perfect, normal family he'd dreamed of them having. The same girl who'd shoved him out of her life and told him never to return.

Determined to bury the images tempting him, he glanced at the clock and muttered. "Where the heck are those kids?"

Isabel was supposed to come straight to *The Gazette* from school. When he'd dropped her off that morning, she'd begged to walk with Kevin, informing him in no uncertain terms – earning a smile, he recalled – it was embarrassing to be picked up by a parent every day.

He shouldn't have given in, but he had, and this was what he got for that one moment of weakness. Nerves wracking him until he saw her sweet face. How much trouble could two kids get into during a ten minute hike? A phone trilled hollowly through the empty office.

Ben grabbed the old fashioned, corded handset from the phone on the cabinet nearest him. "Rosewood Gazette."

"Ben, is Isabel with you?"

His heart plummeted. "No. She's supposed to be coming with Kevin."

"He's here. At Meredith's." A car door slammed. An engine roared to life. "He says she ran away."

Ben nearly dropped the phone. "Ran? But where?"

"She's going to her mother."

"How? She can't–"

"Get to Paris. I know."

Ben cursed. Loud and hard. "She can't have gotten far. I'll check the house in case she went there first."

Before he finished speaking, he was already climbing the stairs out of the basement.

"I'll drive the streets and check the bus stops. She wouldn't get into a car with a stranger, would she?"

"No!" God, he hoped not. "Call if you find her."

"I will." A sharp click ended their connection.

What kind of father was he? He'd brought Isabel to Rosewood to give her something she could count on; the happy life he remembered from his childhood. And somehow, within weeks, he'd failed.

"Please protect my little girl," he whispered to the cloud-filled sky as he emerged from the building and raced for his car.

A short, too fast drive later, he parked in front of their new home. Slamming out of the car, he dashed into the house calling her name. "Isabel. Isabel!"

The house was eerily silent.

"Damn it!"

He was nearly out the door when his cell echoed alongside his jagged breath. He snatched it open.

"I found her."

The sweet sound of Sydney's relief collided with his panic. His knees went weak. "Where is she?"

"At the Trimet bus stop in front of City Hall."

"I'll be right there."

"Ben–"

He pushed the phone closer to his ear, afraid of what Sydney was going to say. Was his baby hurt? Had she been hit by a car? What if she refused to see him, or talk to him? "What?"

Sydney's voice turned gentle. "She's alright. I'll stay with her until you get here. Don't drive so fast you get in an accident on the way."

"I. No. No accident." He shoved his cell into his pocket, sank onto the sofa and dropped his head into shaking hands as fractured breaths racked his body.

How long he sat there like that, he didn't know. All he

knew was he couldn't go collect Isabel with fear and anger raging in his chest.

Thank God Sydney had found her. What would he have done if he'd lost his baby forever? Forcing the crippling thought from his mind, Ben rose, pacing off his anxiety from one end of the living room to the other. When he'd gained quasi-control, his limbs feeling laden, he got into his car, and slowly, carefully drove to City Hall.

So that Sydney and Isabel couldn't see him, he parked behind the building to give himself a few extra minutes to master his still edgy emotions. Knuckles whitening as he gripped the wheel, he acknowledged, grudgingly, it would be poor form to strangle his daughter in public for scaring a hundred years out of his life. Unfortunate, but true. Still that wouldn't stop him from grounding her until she was an old lady.

Finally ready to confront her with some semblance of calm, he crawled out of the car. Rounding City Hall, he found them sitting on a bench, their backs to him. Sydney was bent endearingly close to Isabel.

His steps slowed. He could hear the soft ripple of their voices. Slender, careful fingers, eased the curtain of hair away from Isabel's face. "You know you should apologize to your dad and Kevin, right? You worried them sick. And your dad loves you to pieces. To leave without telling him was a terrible thing to do."

The gentle chastisement took Ben by surprise.

Isabel's response came out puny and glum. "What do you

care? You're leaving tomorrow."

Sydney straightened with a sharp breath. "You're right. I am. But I do care. You're dad–" She paused for a long minute. Ben stood absolutely still, feeling as though a great secret was about to be revealed. "Once upon a time, your dad meant the world to me."

Isabel eyes snapped up to Sydney's. "What happened?"

He waited with bated breath. The truth? He wanted to know too.

"I asked him to leave, and he did."

"Why did you do that?"

Sydney didn't answer. Instead she shrugged; looked down at her hands. So, not the whole truth. His shoulders slumped, the sudden surge of hope for the closure he'd decided long ago he could live without, deflated.

Isabel's shoulders fell with his. She whispered, "I miss my mom."

Sydney's arm wound around his daughter's frail body. "I know you do."

The anger he'd managed to bank moments before flamed partially back to life. He straightened to his full height and blew the fire out. This was no time for pointing fingers. His self-recrimination was hard enough to deal with.

He'd failed Sydney when she needed him the most. Hadn't been strong enough to stand with his high-school sweetheart against her grief. With Isabel he was getting a second chance. And clearly, she was fighting the same grief Sydney had fought – the loss of a parent at too early an age. A parent – despite what he thought of Diana's lack of mothering skills – Isabel loved.

This time he was going to do better. This time he was not going to flake out. This time he was going to stand for his girl; help her learn to be strong when the brutal winds of life's storm knocked her to the ground.

He cleared his throat. Startled, both jerked around. Ben fell head first into the tear-shimmered, clear-brown of Sydney's eyes, and found regret there. Sadness. And a stubborn independence he rather liked.

She nudged Isabel off the bench.

The rush of feet on grass and slender arms circling his waist nearly broke his heart.

"Dad! I'm so sorry." Isabel hiccuped.

He dropped to one knee, smothering his girl in the tightest hug he could without crushing her. "I love you baby-girl. Don't ever do that to me again."

"I won't," she wailed tearfully. "I promise!"

He held her shaking form to his chest. *Thank you,* he mouthed to Sydney.

Ready tears hanging at the edges of her beautiful eyes were dislodged by the jerk of her perfect chin in a curt nod. And then she left him, kneeling in the grass, cradling the child who was the only one who brought any meaning to his life.

At least that's what he repeatedly told himself as he buried his face in his daughter's neck.

NINE

They were tears of gratitude. Really. Syd sat in her car, refusing to look in Ben's direction as he led Isabel off.

Seeing the shattered look on his face when he'd dragged his daughter close to his chest had instantly and vividly taken her back to the day she'd said the worst things possible in order to make him continue on with his plans to leave for college.

Back then, she couldn't let him bury a promising future by staying at his father's lumber yard on her account. She still wouldn't.

It was a long time before she moved, swiping viciously at wet cheeks with the back of her hand. Pulling out her cell, she sucked in a deep breath and placed a call.

"Hello?"

"Hi Meredith. Is Kevin there?"

"He's in the living room with Ben and Isabel. I take it there was a little trouble."

Relief washed through her. "I'll tell you about it when I get back. I'm going to stop at the grocery store and get some things to stock your kitchen."

"What time does your plane leave?"

Meredith sounded exhausted. Syd frowned. "One-thirty."

"I need eggs, milk and some of that fancy cheese from

Ireland. And while you're there, pick up three quarts of Mudslide ice cream."

When the other woman abruptly disconnected, Syd stared at her cell. That couldn't be good. Meredith only indulged in her favorite guilty pleasure when life was giving her a kick in the seat of the pants. Maybe they both needed the gooey pick-me-up. Would three be enough?

The whole time she stalked the isles of the market, she kept telling herself, Meredith would be fine. The insurance company would come through. If there was no word when she got back after shopping, she'd call, make her way up the chain of command if she had to, until she found someone who could make things happen.

When she got on the plane tomorrow, Meredith would be happily taken care of; she could go to New York without worry; and her confusing feelings for Ben would be nothing but a distant memory.

The next morning she let the list of what was left to be done before Grant took her to the airport roll through her mind.

She and Doc had both put in their calls to the insurance company, with the result that the manager in charge of evaluating and implementing benefits was going to personally look into Meredith's case. He'd promised to give them his final verdict this morning.

Unable to sleep, she'd worked into the early hours, putting the rest of her ideas into an outline. Making sure Meredith was sound to sleep, she'd drove to *The Gazette,* fully intending to stay just long enough to leave the file on Ben's desk.

But memories had besieged her determination to leave the old fashioned office and her life in Rosewood behind. The faint, lingering smell of Ben's earthy, sandalwood scent; the comforting silence, knowing the paper had been put to bed for the day with care; the familiar patter of rain on the roof.

She'd closed the door to *The Gazette* behind her for the last time and returned to Meredith's to get whatever sleep she could find for the rest of the night. It wasn't much, and all that was left now was to say good-bye to Isabel. And Ben.

Her stomach did a complicated, nauseating flip. She could do this. A new life waited for her. The lack of a job was just a technicality.

She dropped her carry-on by the front door as someone knocked softly. When she pulled open the door, the man so completely filling her thoughts gave her a sexy, crooked grin. "Didn't think we'd let you leave without saying good-bye did you?"

With a hand pressed against her jittery belly, she stepped back to let Ben and Isabel in. "I was going to come see you."

"Where's Meredith?" Isabel didn't offer a smile.

Syd figured that was the price she had to pay, since her own heart was getting more confused about her departure by the minute. "In the kitchen."

Ben's sharp gaze told her nothing as Isabel closed the door and scooted around them. Syd's skin burned at the blatant sweep over her face. Clearly he was a man with something on his mind.

Too late. In more ways than one. There was nothing left to talk about. She took another step back. "I left my file with the changes we talked about on your desk."

He followed. Too closely. "Found it. Nice work. I'd like to go through it with you later."

The couch hit the back of Syd's thighs as her heartbeat took a flying leap out the window. The house phone rang distantly from another room. Her nerves tangled into a knot, dang it. "Got a plane to catch; world to see, you know?"

Ben left her little room to slip past him without plastering her totally aware self against his tall, muscular frame.

"That's what I want to talk to you about." The deep, quiet timber of his voice, as if she was the only one in the room with him – well actually, she was – held her in place, holding her breath, wondering what could possibly be coming next?

He caught a straggling twist of her hair and bound it between two curious fingers, flipping the end around his thumb. A burn of more than awareness started deep in her belly. "Grant's going to be here any minute."

Ben frowned at her obvious attempt to get him to back off. "Is he taking you to the airport?"

"Yes!" She drew a shaky breath. Finally, he got it. Airport. Plane. Flying away to a more exciting life. Though at the moment, she couldn't envision anything more exciting than putting her hands all over Ben Quincy.

"I'll take you," he said firmly, his burning gaze locked on her lips.

Trap! the magic seeking waif living in her mind shouted.

Biting her lower lip to bring herself back to the sane world, Syd pulled her hair free of his fingers, but then, of its own traitorous accord, her hand flattened on his chest.

He countered with an electric stroke of his finger along the side of her face, tingles of a sharp need she hadn't felt in too long following in its wake.

As though he could read her heart, he said softly, wrapping her in a warm cocoon. "You're needed here."

"No. I'm not."

"Meredith needs you," he said, cheating, then leaned closer still, sending shivers of distracting desire through her. "I didn't get a chance to thank you for finding Isabel. I don't know what I would have done if you hadn't."

He closed the remaining space between them. All thought jumped ship. Syd swayed. Toward him, damn it, but she couldn't turn away from the soft brush of his lips across hers.

Suddenly, she didn't want to escape the strong hands that pulled at her shoulders. Also unfortunate for her, she couldn't bring herself to refuse the slide of his tongue across her lips, or the sexy request for entrance.

The room disappeared. Her plans to board a plane in a few hours got lost amidst the wash of want and heat, and yes, need, that impaled her to the spot.

Somewhere in the distance, banging erupted, but she couldn't be bothered with anything other than the man stroking her back.

Isabel's anxious voice finally broke into Syd's amorous fog. "Dad, come quick. Miss Meredith's banging the phone on the counter. She's breaking it."

Syd broke free. Oh my God! She was kissing Benjamin Quincy and liking it! The thought faded as quickly as it catapulted into her mind. She bolted for the kitchen; found Meredith definitely taking her ire out on the phone.

She gave it a shove, then straightened to her full height, blue eyes blazing. "I'm sorry. Just had to get that out of my system."

Syd pressed her hand to the still rapid pulse at her throat. "What's going on?"

Meredith breathed in deeply, slowly, steadying herself by gripping the counter. "That was the insurance company. My policy doesn't cover in-home care."

Fear hovered deep in her eyes before Meredith managed to hide it. Her feeble hand rose a fraction, as if to wave them off. "Don't worry. Go about your business. I'll be fine. Syd, what time is your plane?"

She didn't have the heart to tell the other woman they'd talked about it yesterday. "One-thirty."

"Well, you'd better get going. It's a long drive, and there's security to get through." Meredith's voice trailed off as she swayed. Her eyes glazed.

Syd rushed to grab her, but Ben beat her to it. She pulled the on closest chair, positioning it under Meredith's bottom.

Eyes clearing, the slack look on her face eased. "I'm

okay."

"You don't look okay. Isabel, take my cell and call the Doc." Syd took a shuddering breath. *Stay calm.*

She'd just had a make out session that would make the pages of a steamy novel burn to a crisp. She was due to board a plane within the next few hours. And here she stood shoulder to shoulder with Ben, Isabel joining them after making the call, hovering protectively over Meredith, who was as much a part of her family as her own mother.

If she weren't so scared and panicked–

All over again, she stood at her father's bedside, watching him struggle with his illness and looming mortality. Tears she refused to let fall gathered at the corners of her eyes.

How could she leave? How was she going to be happy in a job thousands of miles away, knowing Meredith needed her more than she needed that stupid job?

Isabel anxiously clung to Meredith. Ben's reassuring hand found a way to Syd's shoulder. His warm breath brushed the hair at her temple.

"Let's move you to the couch." His deep baritone was directed at Meredith, but it sent shivers down Syd's spine. Here was a man who knew what to do. Had she known that about him back when life had pitched her a curve ball she couldn't hit?

"Don't be silly. I'll just sit here for a moment." The slurring left Meredith's voice.

In that instant, the whole thing – her lack of the perfect job, her impending departure, the magic she was looking to reclaim – it all faded into the background, and what was most important became quite simple and straightforward.

She wasn't getting on that plane. Not that she was giving up her dream. It'd been hanging on for a long time and wasn't going anywhere. But the simple facts were, Meredith needed her, and she wasn't going to repeat the mistake she'd made of leaving her dad when all she had left with him was a small stretch of time.

Syd pressed a kiss to Meredith's temple. "I'll stay with you."

A tired, dispirited look crawled across the other woman's pale face. "I know I've been angling for just that, but I don't want you to stay because of me. What I've got can't be easily fixed. And you've got your whole life ahead of you."

"Hush, now. I've decided. We're not going to talk about it anymore." The front door opened and closed. "There's the Doc."

~*~

"Tell me about your teachers. Do you like them?"

Syd's question was aimed at Isabel, but her anxious gaze kept darting down the hall to the bedroom where the Doc had taken Meredith.

Ben glanced at the clock. She was going to miss her plane, and after their bone rattling kiss earlier, he wasn't sure how he felt about that. He hadn't followed in his father's footsteps, but the one thing his dad had that he wanted most, was a happy, normal family.

His parents didn't live in Rosewood anymore. They'd sold

the lumber yard and moved to Florida, taking his younger brother and sister with them. Randall was a detective in the local police department. Jocelyn was in college, studying to be a Physician's Assistant.

As a family, they spanned the country, but Ben had known for a long time he wouldn't follow them to the east coast. Despite all that had happened, his heart would always call Rosewood home.

So here he was. With his daughter. Trying to make a home for them in the one place where, except for the one time, life had been good.

But there was nothing normal about his life since Sydney had cut him loose and he'd fathered a child with another woman. And there was nothing normal about the feelings that crowded him for the lady worrying her heart out for her ex-boss.

When he'd come this morning, he'd had some vague idea of talking her into staying. But not like this. He glanced at the clock again. She could still make it if they left this very minute.

From painful experience, he suspected she wouldn't leave now. And a part of the heart he'd walled off cracked open. God, he was in real danger here. But hers was the greater danger.

The haze of lust – that's all it could possibly be – cleared. If she stayed, Sydney would lose the one thing she craved the most. The freedom to soar high into the sun. It didn't take a conk upside the head to realize he couldn't let that happen.

His first priority was Isabel and what *she* needed. But not at the expense of Sydney's dream.

Doc Tucker emerged from the hall leading to Meredith's room and went straight to Sydney. In a few long strides, Ben was at her back offering silent support. He reached for Isabel.

At the feel of her small hand in his, he knew what he had to do. He had his dream. Sydney had hers. As much as he did, she deserved to reach for the stars and find the prize waiting.

"Meredith?"

"She's overtired, but going to be fine. I'll write an order for physical therapy to help build her strength." Doc frowned at Sydney. "Aren't you supposed to be on your way to New York?"

Sydney shook her head. Before she could tell Doc she wasn't going, Ben turned her to face him. "If we leave right now, you can still make your plane."

The corners of her sweet lips turned up. "If you drive like a maniac." The teasing smile died. "I already called Grady and told him I wasn't flying out today. Is the job you offered still available?"

Doc's bushy brows rose. His aging eyes lit with curiosity.

Ben dug in his heels. "You want to go to New York."

"I want to stay with Meredith." Her chin elevated. "So, are you taking back your offer?"

He tried to spit out a resounding *yes*, but with her beautiful eyes lit with determination, and the soft curve of her chin angled to argue with him, he couldn't. "No. If you want the job, it's yours."

He tried one last time to get her on that damn plane. "The wages won't be what you'd make in New York, or at some other glossy magazine."

She shrugged one graceful shoulder, her fiery gaze promising a battle if he didn't fall in line. "I don't need much. And I can supplement whatever you pay with freelance work."

He'd never once doubted Sydney's fighting spirit, only who she thought the enemy was. The woman facing him with fists perched on her shapely hips was not the same scared girl who'd sent him away all those years ago. His gut skittered in appreciation.

Doc chuckled, grabbed his medical bag and headed for the door, but not before sending a wink in Ben's direction. "Sounds like you two have some things to work out. Call my office this afternoon and Lucy will give you the information for scheduling Meredith's physical therapy."

The door closed quietly behind the still chuckling older man. Beside Ben, Isabel gaped at Sydney. "You're not leaving?"

The stubborn woman shifted her gaze to his daughter before she let her fists drop. "No. I'm going to stay and help Meredith get better."

"Can I help too?"

Sydney shot him a quizzical look. "I guess that's up to your dad."

Isabel tugged on his arm until he transferred his gaze to her. "Can I, dad?"

"Of course you can."

"What should I do first?"

Ben raised brows at Sydney. She ran a gentle hand on Isabel's hair. If he'd thought he was in trouble earlier, it was nothing compared to the quagmire he found himself in now. "There's a pitcher on the counter. Can you fill it with water and take it, and a glass to Meredith?"

Isabel gave a little excited hop. "Sure."

As his daughter disappeared into the kitchen, Sydney met his searching gaze with an unbending stare of her own. If she thought for one second, he couldn't see past the defenses she was busy erecting; that he would cave like he did the last time, then it was time to disabuse her of the notion. "I'm amending my offer."

She went perfectly still, the clear brown of her eyes turning dark and muddy. "You are?"

"I'll hire Clare Marsh like I promised, but I want you to keep looking for the job you really want."

"I didn't say I wasn't going to."

"Just making it clear. I don't want to be the one keeping you chained to Rosewood."

Her pretty face lost all expression. "You want me to leave."

It was easy enough to guess what was churning around in that gorgeous head of hers. Ben narrowed his eyes on the woman. He didn't like feeling like a jerk, but he let her think what she wanted – that he was giving her the bum's rush. She should recognize the maneuver.

"That was your plan."

Eleven years ago, she'd been so scared she couldn't let him help her. This time it would be different. He was under no illusions that she would accept his assistance, so he'd make sure she left no stone unturned, even if it meant submitting applications behind her back. What she didn't know wouldn't hurt her.

But from the set of Sydney's slender shoulders, his guess was, he'd just lost his kissing privileges, not that he'd had any, but damn. It wasn't going to be easy to forget how right she'd felt in the shelter of his arms.

TEN

Syd moved through the rest of the day wrapped in a fog. She didn't know what was worse, missing her flight – even though she had no regrets about her decision – or finding out Ben was so desperate to get her on the plane, he'd insisted on taking her himself.

Of course he wants you to leave. It's the least you deserve after sending him away, and then kissing him as though there was no tomorrow.

With a sigh, she settled tiredly into the welcome silence of Meredith's family room and leaned back into the over-stuffed loveseat. She closed her eyes. As soon as Meredith no longer needed her, she would go.

A familiar woody scent tickled her nose, sending trickles of awareness racing along her skin. The cushion beside her shifted under new weight.

Syd didn't bother opening her eyes. "What are you doing here?"

"Meredith promised Isabel a game of Scrabble. We brought desert."

The things Ben's deep voice did to her...she didn't dare think about it. "What kind of desert?"

"Vanilla ice cream on warm brownies." A bowl bumped her arm. "Better eat quick before the ice cream melts."

After the day she'd had, she couldn't be bothered to do more than stay right where she was. But seduced by the smell of sweet vanilla and warm chocolate wrapped in Ben's charm? She took his offering, with a silent caution to watch her step where the tempting man was concerned.

His leg brushed hers, snapping her half-asleep senses wide-awake. "How are you doing?"

It wasn't the casual *hi-how-are-you-doing* greeting of one friend to another, but a probe she was too numb, and hyper-aware of how physically close he was, to fend off.

"I called my landlady in New York and told her I wasn't going to need the apartment, and why. I won't get all of the deposit back, but most of it, because she said she had someone ready to move in."

"Where's your boyfriend? Why isn't he here with you?"

The questions were growled low. The sensual taste of warm ice cream, mixed with the perfect brownie, kept her distracted as she tried not to think about what it would be like to spoon feed the man sitting too close.

She swallowed the sweet desert. "Boyfriend?"

"That guy from Rose's. Grant Reed. Why isn't he here?"

Syd face Ben, her knee bumping his, shooting a flare of startling anticipation straight to places she would prefer didn't notice. He was frowning fiercely at her.

Not surprised at his assumption, since she was the one who'd fostered it, she cleared her throat, a little astonished someone – her mother or Meredith, except Meredith had been kind of busy – hadn't set him straight.

"Grant isn't my boyfriend."

"Does he know that?"

"Of course, he does." Wobbling nerves put a squeak in her voice. She trapped her thick hair in one hand.

Ben put his bowl on the coffee table, angled to face her, tangling their legs enough to short circuit every coherent thought she might have managed. "That's not what it looked like to me."

Which had been the whole point of Grant's antics.

Something unexpected stirred in the depths of his grey eyes as they roamed over her face. Syd snapped her guard in place.

"Where are you going to stay?" *Now that you're not leaving.*

He didn't have to say it; she got the silent message. Self defense had her chin rising sharply. "With Meredith."

His shuttered expression softened. Suspicion straightened her back. She wasn't looking for anything from Ben, least of all charitable forgiveness. "Tell me about Isabel's mother."

He eased back. She breathed easier. Kind of.

"There's not much to tell. Diana is...a fashion designer. She lives in Paris with her husband."

Syd's mind bounced back to their reckless clutch that morning. What the man could do with his lips should be made illegal. She wished it was the old attraction undermining her ability to laugh off the sudden need to grab his shirt-front and reel him in, but she couldn't.

Fighting desire with fire, she opened the lid to the anger coming to a boil in her chest. "Why didn't she take Isabel with her? What mother would leave her child behind?"

Tugging until she let loose of her hair, strong, capable fingers tangled in the ringlets along one side of her face. Ben's lips curled into a hard smile. "It was a mutual decision. I wanted Isabel to stay with me. She wanted to focus on her career and new husband."

His hand slipped to the nape of her neck and drew her close.

Having little resistance left, Syd swallowed hard. Ben didn't know she'd followed him to Chicago and what it'd cost her.

She pushed on his chest. Wiping all emotion from her voice, she whispered, "This isn't a good idea."

The mouth that had been about to overpower her battlements twisted into a self-deprecating slash across his handsome face. "Don't I know it."

~*~

Ben ushered a sleepy Isabel up to her bedroom. Despite the short ride, she'd fallen asleep in the car. The darkened room was lit by moonlight through the newly curtained window. He barely had the covers pulled back before she flopped on the bed.

Removing her shoes, he didn't bother insisting she change into pj's, instead tucked her in, then sat on the floor, his back to the wall as he watched her sleep.

Kissing Sydney was the dumbest move he'd made since

moving back to Rosewood. It ranked right in there with expecting their life to turn into Mayberry R.F.D. What in the hell was he thinking? Not with his brain, that was for sure.

Shoving his hands through his hair, he swore under his breath. Why couldn't he keep his hands off? Over the years, he'd met prettier girls, had tried to make relationships with one or two who tugged on his senses. None of them would have put their lifelong dream on hold to help a friend the way Sydney had that day.

The last time he'd had so little control of his heart and soul, it'd ended in disaster. The very last thing he wanted was another trouncing.

He was a single dad doing the best he knew how for a troubled daughter, who needed help navigating life's rocky slopes. And he had an outdated newspaper to renovate and make financially viable.

Nothing could be more important than that. Not the ridiculous spark of jealousy that reared up when he'd been confronted with the possibility of another man in Sydney's life, and certainly not this irreverent attraction for the worst possible girl in Rosewood.

They were friends. Friends with a past, but it didn't matter. *Stick to the plan, man.*

The next morning he consumed a full pot of full-leaded coffee while unpacking boxes as he waited for Isabel to surface. His restless dreams had been filled with images of Sydney, a running tableau of her as a serious teenager one minute. A beautiful woman cradled carefully in his arms, his hands skimming hungrily over her soft skin, the next.

Between the dreams and his excited state when he'd finally woke in the early hours with little enough sleep, he'd made up his mind to leave the past where it belonged. Behind him.

He would apologize for his recent misbehavior, but other than that, Sydney Marshall, AKA Clare Marsh was only a colleague assisting him in the updating of his business. In return, he would pay her a decent wage and put feelers out for a job she couldn't turn down.

Isabel stumbled into the kitchen. He set her up at the table with a bowl of cereal. "How about we go for a hike today."

"Can Sydney come with us?"

Not part of the plan. "She has to stay with Meredith." Isabel's shoulders sank in disappointment, but Ben held his ground. "I thought we'd spend the weekend exploring Rosewood. Get acquainted with our new home."

Isabel gave him one of her infamous *duh* looks. "That should take ten minutes. It's not a very big town, Dad."

"Sassy pants." He pulled gently on a lank of hair. "We can start with exploring Mill River Dam."

That perked her up. "There's a dam in Rosewood?"

Ben smiled. "Uh huh. Upriver a little ways. We can have a picnic."

His heart warmed at her sudden grin. "Sweet."

"Finish breakfast and go get ready. Wear something besides black," he instructed dryly.

Isabel wrinkled her nose, but when she came out of her bedroom, he stopped loading their lunch sack with the sandwiches he'd made. Hair pulled back in a ponytail, she wore a plain, pink tee-shirt with green shorts. Her sweet face was scrubbed clean of the makeup he hadn't yet been able to find. Miraculously, his daughter looked like a normal ten year old.

He winked at her, earning a pretty blush. Maybe he was doing the right thing after all.

"About ready." He finished loading the sack. "I have one errand to run on the way."

When he stopped in front of Meredith's, Isabel bounced, unhooking her seat belt. "I'm coming in too."

"No need to. This will only take a second."

But, Isabel was out of the car in a flash, racing for the house. Shaking his head, Ben killed the engine. The last thing he needed was an audience.

By the time he caught up with his speedy daughter, Sydney was answering the door. Her smile was all for Isabel. "Hi. What brings you guys here?"

The arched look she tossed him over his daughter's head was cautious. He didn't blame her. He'd been giving her mixed signals. Which was why he had to get this over with.

"We're going to Mill River Dam for a picnic," Isabel gushed as she pushed past Sydney.

"Isabel. Manners," he scolded.

"Sorry," she grinned lopsidedly over her shoulder as she headed to Meredith's room.

"Sorry about that. She's excited."

Sydney stepped back, granting him entrance. Her lips quirked in a quick smile. His pulse took a giant leap. "No problem. I would be excited too."

He followed her into the great-room meant to be filled with a family. He ignored the thought. "Look, I want to apologize."

Isabel returned immediately from the back part of the house. "Where's Meredith?"

Sydney's startled gaze darted to his daughter. "She went with my mother to Rose's Bakery. They have breakfast there every Saturday. After, they go shopping."

Crowded by a randy desire to repeat the lip-lock he was attempting to apologize for, Ben moved further into the room away from the woman taking over too much of his mind and space. A book lay face down on the couch, lap blanket tossed carelessly to the side, and a half empty cup of tea caught his eye on the end table.

He frowned. Clearly Sydney wasn't hanging out, waiting for him to come out and play.

Isabel demanded. "When will they be back?"

Sydney shrugged, keeping her eyes on his daughter. "Sometime this afternoon. Before Meredith gets too tired would be my guess."

Something perverse in Ben raised its contrary head, mostly so she'd look at him. "Do you want to come with us?"

He could have bit his tongue, but it was too late.

Sydney's gaze shifted to him. *Ah, there you are,* he said

silently with smug satisfaction.

"I don't think so, but thanks for the invitation."

"Yes! Please come with us." Isabel did a quick two step and grabbed Sydney's hand. When she still hesitated, Isa made sweet puppy-dog eyes and begged, "Please?"

Boy, the brat was good. No one with a heart as big as Sydney's could say no to that.

"I packed plenty of food," he admitted, adding incentive.

He'd stopped by to apologize so he could put some distance between them. Instead he was asking her to go on a picnic. It didn't make sense, but what the heck. He was done fighting the impulse to spend time with the impossible woman.

"Well–" Confusion filled the startling eyes that still had the power to wobble his world. "Okay."

"Good. Let's go then."

A blue, cloudless sky kept them company on the short ride to the dam, which was completed, on Ben's part, in silence. The girls chattered like magpies.

He couldn't remember the last time Isabel had been so animated. "Dad's going to get me a saxophone."

He felt Sydney's curiosity as she shifted to look at him, but he couldn't afford the price of getting caught in the web of attraction he should have been working harder to ignore.

He parked the Camaro by a path that led through a covered walking bridge to metal stairs winding up to the dam. The faint smell of vanilla scuttled him, making him acutely aware of the woman's every move. As a matter of self-preservation, he pretended he didn't notice.

Sydney turned back to his daughter. "Do you like band?"

Isabel sighed heavily. "The teacher's letting me borrow a sax until Dad gets mine, but learning to play it is really hard."

Ben grabbed the lunch bag. "This is your first try at a musical instrument. It's bound to be a little difficult."

"My mind and fingers don't want to work together," his girl groused in typical Isabel fashion.

Ben risked a smile when she scampered up the stairs ahead of them.

"What if you think about the notes as math equations?" Sydney suggested, pausing halfway.

"Maybe," Isabel shrugged, then sprinted the rest of the way to the top.

Who was this woman? Not the same girl who'd callously cut him out of her life. He cleared his throat, gently grabbing her arm. "Wait a sec. I...um...want to apologize for my...behavior yesterday."

She stopped, her breath huffing out between parted lips, chest rising and falling. Delicate brows arched in question. Lips formed a small kissable *oh*, as she caught on.

A gentle breeze ruffled her hair. Ben cut off the arousal tempting him to repeat the behavior he was supposed to be regretting. "I shouldn't have kissed you."

"Why? Was it awful?"

"Hell no," he sputtered, then quickly regained his equilibrium. "I didn't mean it is all."

When her brows snapped together, he swallowed a string

of swear words. This was getting worse by the minute. Her pretty face went blank. She took the next step up the stairs, putting frosty brown eyes on level with his. "I see."

"I didn't mean that like it sounded."

"What did you mean?" Her tone couldn't have been colder if they were having this discussion at the North Pole, in sub-zero temperatures.

He tried again. "Just that you were right. It wasn't a good idea. We're colleagues. We should keep it that way. That's all I meant."

Isabel appeared at the top. "Hey. You guys coming? I'm hungry."

He waved at his daughter. "We'll be right there."

"Colleagues. Of course. No problem."

Sydney resumed climbing, her back stiff, hips teasing him with a tantalizing swing. Now that he'd got that out of the way, he could forget there had been a time when he'd believed their future was tied together a perfect, big red bow.

~*~

A maniacal laugh erupted quietly from Syd's throat. Well, probably not maniacal, but the bubble welling in her chest felt pretty darn close. She tossed the steno pad she was making notes in on the desk, and rocked back in the chair. Naturally the weather outside the window matched her mood. Dark and drizzling.

As apologies went, Ben's for kissing her socks off sucked. Big time. And if he was so sorry he'd rocked her universe, what was the ice cream and brownie all about the night she'd missed her plane?

She'd thought he was trying to make her feel better, not that she needed it. She'd made her decision with a clear heart and mind, but she *had* felt better, dang it. And had been sweetly surprised when he'd insisted she go on a picnic with him and his daughter, a girl who needed a woman's influence more than any child Syd had ever seen.

In fact, Isabel reminded her so much of herself at a much older age – lost, and bitterly lonely – she didn't know if she should laugh or cry.

Huffing out an exasperated breath, she rocked the chair forward, jumped to her feet, and paced the length of the room. She wasn't expecting anything from Ben. They were water under the bridge. As he so earnestly pointed out, colleagues, working together to save a rundown, town institution. Nothing more.

Which was why her solution to the feelings swirling in her chest – not disappointment, she was quick to point out to her weary heart – was to put her nose to the grindstone and herself into the work Ben was paying her for. And she'd watched over Meredith, only letting the other woman out of her sight when her mother came and the two escaped on short excursions to keep Meredith's sanity and her mind off her slow recovery.

Methodically Syd had put the final polish on the article about the auditors who'd been hired by the town council to go through the city books. The completed grant request, which she'd added to her stack of things to do, sat at her elbow ready to be mailed. And, she was waiting for the last of the advertisers for Friday's edition to give her the go ahead.

While she played the roll of Girl Friday, Syd did her best to forgot that once-upon-a-time, long ago, this attraction for a certain male making havoc of her emotions had been as natural to her as breathing.

She paced back to the window behind the desk. The joke was on her, but it was no laughing matter. She'd wanted excitement. And she'd gotten it in the form of Ben Quincy and his imp of a daughter.

Voices at the front of the house startled her. Before she could investigate, Grant stuck his head in the office, an urber-satisfied grin splitting his face. "Time for a break. I brought goodies...and news."

Grabbing her hand, he dragged her to the kitchen where everyone was gathered.

"What kind of news?"

Ben stood on the other side of Isabel frowning at their clasped hands. Syd wasn't surprised by the smug smile Grant shot in Ben's direction before leaning close to her ear.

Her face went hot. Smacking his shoulder, she jerked her hand free and hissed, "Stop it. What news?"

His laugh was full of mischief, the scamp. "The good news is, I'm taking a vacation."

She stared at her best friend. It wasn't that he *never* took vacations, only – she glance furtively at Ben – why now? "What? When? And what about your grandma?"

"I'm going to a Star Trek convention in Reno. I made all

the arrangements this morning. An intern from the Oregon Culinary Institute is coming in to help Grandma for a couple of weeks."

"A couple of weeks?"

"After the convention, I've decided to take some time off and go to Belize."

The popular travel destination was on her list of most interesting places to go, not Grant's. "What are you going to do there?"

He wiggled his brows. "Whatever tourists do?"

"When are you leaving?"

He blocked Ben's scowling visage. "Tomorrow."

"So soon?"

Grant grinned. "The bad news is you can't go. You get to stay here and play co-chair of the new library fund-raising committee with your pal, Ben Quincy."

"Says who?"

Grant eased aside until she could see Meredith and her mother peering into one of the pastry boxes with Isabel.

"You're kidding, right?"

"'Fraid not, Slick." He rewarded her frown with a friendly kiss on her temple. "I have faith you'll handle it just fine."

Ben leaned over Isabel's shoulder, scowling as though he wanted to pitch the box of pastries into next week.

"You want to bet?"

"Tell me how it all goes when I get back."

He moved off to open the second box on the counter.

Meredith swayed before catching herself with a grip on the counter. With a harried breath, Syd hurried to stand next to her, just in case. Reaching for the lone maple bar – for Meredith, it was her favorite – she bumped fingers with Ben over the luscious sugary confection. Her stomach took a tumble, and not from lack of feeding her carb addiction.

Grabbing her hand back, she started to stammer, then cleared her throat enough to speak as if the accidental touching of their fingers had not inspired a serious tremor in her world. "You take it."

"I'm sure there's more in the other box." Ben moved off.

Her skin flushed hot. A hard kick in the shin would do them both good. But to be fair, she couldn't blame Ben. It wasn't his fault that in this room filled with those she considered friends and family, she still felt a tiny pang of loneliness at his dismissive tone.

Startled at the direction her thoughts were taking, she made sure Meredith had everything she needed, and with confusion turning the sugar in her mouth sour, carried her apple fritter to the table.

Her mother sat across from her, giving Syd no time to catch her breath. "We're forming a committee to raise funds for the new library."

"And you want me and Ben to co-chair."

Lauren sipped her tea, watching closely, "Grant let the cat out of the bag?"

"He did."

Her mother enthused over the project; all the ways they

could raise money for the new library Rosewood was so desperately in need of. The cloying smell of sweet baked goods make Syd a little dizzy, as she let her gaze brush by the man wrecking her not-so-peaceful morning, to settle instead on Isabel.

The truth was, while Ben had made this wonderful little girl with the other woman, she'd never gotten over him. She thought she'd managed to strip away the memories of how happy she'd been, before high school, to let his friendship fill her days. How, before her father's illness, she'd begun to believe loving him could take up the rest of her life. But she obviously hadn't.

Syd took the startling hit on the chin, then straightened in her chair. She could put her big girl panties on with the best of them. There *was* no going back. She knew that. Knew she couldn't change what had happened, or the fallout. All she could do was what Ben was paying her to do.

An idea suddenly stilled her tumbling thoughts. Perhaps there was something...

Since it appeared she was going to be in Rosewood for a little while longer, she could think of *one* thing she could accomplish. And oddly enough, she knew right where to start.

ELEVEN

"Why not let Isabel tutor math?" Syd demanded.

It was Friday night, and Ben was driving them to the football game, where they were to meet Isabel, Meredith, and Syd's mother. Rosewood was playing La Salle in a rivalry of long standing.

Usually Grant went with her to the games, but the rat had skipped out; jumping a plane, leaving her all alone to unravel the knot her life had tangled into.

"She's ten years old. That's not old enough to tutor other kids."

"Ben, she's a genius. Of course she can tutor. I'll be right there, in case she needs help." And keeping the vow she'd secretly made to help his daughter acclimate to her new home.

His mouth firmed into a slash across his handsome face. "You don't have to tell *me* how smart she is."

The man could growl all he wanted. His reluctance was not going to change her mind. Allowing Isabel to tutor math could give him what he wanted most.

She balled her hands into fists on her lap. Okay, she was doing this for Isabel, but there was a slight chance she was doing it more for Ben. And it wasn't going well.

Syd shifted within the confines of the seat belt so she could look directly at the man stealing beneath her unsteady defenses. "If you want her to be happy, tutoring is a wonderful way to make new friends."

Glaring at her, he braked hard at the stop sign. "Did she say she wasn't happy?"

"Not exactly."

"What do you mean, then?"

Against her better judgment, something long forgotten went squishy in her chest. Ben was a really good dad. She should know. Her own dad had been the best. "She hasn't come right out and said she isn't happy."

A horn honked behind them. Just short of ringing her neck, Syd figured, Ben faced forward, eased up on the brake, letting the Camaro roll through the four-way stop. "Well, I think it's best to concentrate on one thing at a time. I'm sure she'll make friends with the other band members."

Syd let go of the dashboard she'd grabbed at his sudden stop. "How's the sax practice going?"

His hands relaxed on the wheel. One corner of his mouth twitched. "I didn't know a sax could sound...quite like that."

"She plays for Meredith. She's trying very hard."

"She is," he acknowledged softly, with more than a little fatherly pride.

Her heart skipped before dancing a ridiculous jitterbug. "When's her first recital?"

His wary gaze snapping back to her, Ben parked the car. "You're planning to go?"

Syd shrugged, growing uncomfortable with the new intimacy drawing her closer than she wanted to be to the man she'd once pushed away. This ground was dangerous. Feeling a part of what Ben was building for his family of two could be disastrous.

If she wasn't careful, the last time they'd split was going to seem like a walk in the park in comparison to how much this would hurt when she left them to go on with her career. "Isabel invited me."

Growing tension snapped between them, a high powered electric line. He paused with his hand on the door handle, one brow hitched. "Have you gotten any nibbles on your resume?"

Her skin flushed with warmth. *Nibbles?*

The only nibbles she wanted–

"Um, not yet," she stumbled.

"Her recital is next Wednesday."

Syd took a deep breath as she exited Ben's ride. *Dangerous ground. Watch your step, girl.*

~*~

Ben scooted to make room for the woman rapidly getting under his skin. Keep it professional. That was the rule.

The problem with having rules was the smell of vanilla that was specifically Sydney's, mixing with the sizzle of the hot dogs and fries he'd bought on the way to their seats; the twist of her hair as it lay along the sides of her gamin face and curled around her jaw, begging for his touch; the fit of her jeans, and the soft sway of her hips as he'd followed her in from the parking lot.

He shook his head to clear it of the flood of arousal. When she sat next to him, her leg brushed his, giving his decision a kick in the proverbial butt. Thankfully, Isabel chose that moment to bounce onto the bleachers and plop down on his other side.

"Kevin's playing tonight," she happily informed him.

Mentally, Ben patted himself on the back. Despite what Sydney had said in the car, his daughter *was* having fun. The small things mattered in Rosewood. Friday night football at the high school, where your friend was a wide receiver on the junior varsity team, was one of them.

Feeling a smug tug at the little success, he took Meredith's hand and steadied her as she navigated the squeaky bleachers to their second row seats. Lauren had a hand on her other arm.

When Sydney moved to make room for both women between them, Meredith waived her back with a artful smile. "No, no, you stay where you are. I'll sit over there."

Ben shook his head. The older woman's penchant for throwing them together was blatantly obvious, but he didn't need anyone managing his love life. Not that he had one. And certainly not with Sydney Marshall. What he needed was to stop looking at the gorgeous woman like she was the choicest cut in a freezer filled with lesser stakes.

Meredith wobbled as she inched to Syd's other side. They both grabbed for the rascally older woman.

"Falling not allowed," Sydney quipped.

The concern hiding beneath the sassy words of warning settled in Ben's chest, attacking the one organ he didn't dare let the woman near. But then, she would do something so incredibly perfect, like fuss over Meredith; insist on finding a way for Isabel to fit in at her new school.

He needed a retraining bolt! Ben sat his soda on the bench with a little too much force. The drink nearly toppled off the bleachers and into the dirt below before he rescued it.

"Dad, look! There's Kevin."

The JV team ran onto the field. Isabel clapped her hands and cheered at the top of her lungs. Ben rubbed his ringing ear.

Sydney grinned at Isabel's exuberance, and his heart did a very bad thing. It twisted into a clumsy somersault.

"Oh I forgot–" Meredith leaned across Sydney, holding out a postcard. A troubled look flit across the older woman's face. "This came for Isabel today."

He took it, was slow in recognizing the well-known tower surrounded by city lights on the front side, but knew the writing on the back. Before he could get it out of sight, Isabel, who'd glanced over as Meredith passed along the postcard, saw her name in the address.

"For me?"

When he nodded, she snatched it from him, turning it over and over until she stopped to read the short message. She flipped the postcard one more time to stare at the Eiffel Tower. Her new found joy leached from her sweet face, leaving her looking more fragile than ever. "It's from Mom."

Ben wrapped his arm around her slumped shoulders, tried the high road, though his irritation with Diana soared to new heights. She could have waited a little longer before disturbing their peace. "I see that, baby. Is she having a good time?"

"I guess." Isabel's chin quivered, all delight in the game gone.

Sydney reached across his lap, her softness pushing into his shoulder as she gently encased Isabel's arm in compassionate fingers. "What does she say?"

Hell yes, he was in deep trouble.

Tears glistened in his little girl's eyes. Feeling helpless, he pressed his lips to the top of her head.

"Her first show went spectacularly well, and...and she's glad I'm here with Dad." Isabel's shoulders shook once, before she sucked in a breath, biting her lower lip. "She doesn't have time for me."

Ben shifted quickly to her other side. He couldn't contend with her tears and Sydney's tantalizing body leaning into his, all at the same time. And Isabel needed him more than he needed to pull the provocative woman into his arms for a spine tingling necking session.

But the move was a mistake, because Sydney closed ranks with him and together they sandwiched Isabel protectively between them. It felt too intimate, the two of them bracketing his grieving daughter, making them three.

Ben shook off the feeling, wishing he could find the right words to soothe away her misery. "Your mom knows your home is here now. And she wants you to be happy."

"I want to be with her sooo bad," Isabel hiccuped.

Sydney tucked Isabel's hair behind her ear. "You can't

leave now. Your dad needs your help at the paper, and your first band recital is next week."

"I suck at playing the sax. It's a stupid instrument. I'll never learn to play it in time." The words rushed out in a crippled whisper.

Feeling as worthless a crumbs left on a table, and desperate too, he looked over Isabel's bowed head at Sydney. Her brows rose, along with her shoulders in a helpless shrug.

How was he going to make living in Rosewood seem as much fun as going to Paris with Diana? He grabbed at the last thing he and Sydney had been discussing. "Sydney was wondering if you wanted to tutor Math."

Isabel wiped her eyes with her fingers. "Tutor?"

Sydney took Isabel's hand. "I'll help you. I tutor reading."

Isabel wrinkled her nose.

"You'll like it, I promise."

His gaze snapped to the woman looking at his girl as if she meant every word she said. When they were younger, she'd made promises to him, too. Promises of friendship, if not fidelity. Promises of a life together that would last longer that the time it took to change her mind.

What would he do if she broke this promise?

Tightening his arm around Isabel's crumpled shoulders, he drew her against his chest, away from the woman who'd completely changed the direction he'd thought his life would go. "You and I will go to the counselor's office on Monday morning and look into it. How does that sound?"

Sydney's gaze shot to his. The hurt shining in her

beautiful eyes at his exclusion made him feel small, but damn it! He had to protect Isabel.

By the time the game was done, and the home team had won, Isabel's spirits were semi-restored, but Sydney had remained quiet throughout, her turbulent gaze locked on the field.

Ben cursed soundly under his breath. He hadn't meant to take his frustration out on her, he just wanted to keep her at the periphery of their lives, so he could stay focused on why he'd brought Isabel to his hometown in the first place.

He locked his jaw, refusing to feel bad about his decision.

On the field, Kevin high-fived his teammates as they left the field. There was no varsity game scheduled to follow. Ben searched the remaining crowd, looking for the boy's parents. No one was waiting on the sideline, cheering him home.

"Dad, can I go with Meredith?"

He glanced at Isabel. "Sure. Another game of Scrabble?"

She nodded, her good humor somewhat restored. Kevin reached their small group, while Sydney still refused to meet his gaze.

"Nice touchdown in the third quarter, son." Ben winced at the unfortunate phrasing.

Kevin's ears turned red. "Thanks."

Feeling for the kid, Ben slapped a hand on the boy's shoulder. "See you at the paper after school on Monday?"

Kevin jerked away. "Sure. Gotta go. See you in school," he said to Isabel, then took off at a run.

Disturbed at Kevin's sudden departure, and catching

Sydney's worried look, he knuckled the top of Isabel's head. "Go. Have fun with Meredith. I'll pick you up later."

She scampered off, easily catching up as Lauren carefully ushered Meredith toward the parking lot.

Sydney's sudden nervousness shimmered in the night air. "I'd better leave, too. I can catch a ride with Mom."

He placed a staying hand on her arm. "I'll take you home."

Immediately, like leaves flying before a feisty breeze, that astounding tug and pull between them scattered whatever else he might have said.

Let her go, Quincy. Ben let his hand fall to his side. "It seems I'm always apologizing to you. I didn't mean to be hurtful earlier."

Sydney stepped off the bleachers, wobbling a little once she got to the ground. "I get it. I do. I'm leaving soon. And you're trying to make a home for Isabel. I thought I could help. But, it's okay if you don't want me to."

Sucker punched, Ben caught her, steering toward the track around the outside of the football field. "Walk with me?"

She pulled free and folded her arms around her rib cage with a shiver. Taking off his hoodie, he draped it over her shoulders, making sure his fingers didn't linger at the place where her slender neck joined her shoulders.

"You'll get cold," she protested, but he ignored the husky concern in her voice.

"How's the job hunt going?"

Grasping the edges of the sweatshirt, she pulled them

together and shrugged. "No bites yet, but I'm sure something will turn up."

They walked side by side, the silence becoming unexpectedly companionable. Their shoulders brushed every few steps. The seduction of her favorite scent, the fleeting worry over a boy who should have been nothing more than a student she was teaching to read, wouldn't leave him alone.

He put more space between them. "What do you think is going on with Kevin?"

"I don't know." She frowned at her feet.

He wished she'd look at him, because then he could tell her not to worry; that everything would be okay with the boy. He hoped.

Pushing a hand through his hair, he blurted, "What exactly are you looking for?"

If he knew, he could help her find it. A crazy thought. The craziest he'd ever had.

"Magic." The word came out in a breathless rush, as though she didn't have to give any thought to it.

"Magic," he repeated, not quite understanding.

Her short bark of laughter was brittle. When she finally looked at him, the goal post loomed behind her. "I know. It's silly."

Leashed anger pushed its way out of the closet, where for so long, he'd kept it locked away. "There's magic here. In Rosewood. Always has been. Eleven years ago, you cast it aside. Said we were through."

He couldn't believe he'd kept count of every year that had

passed.

"We were. Are." She took a step away. "Whatever we had back then died, while I sat at my Dad's beside and watched cancer take him away."

Unable to push the anger back where it'd sprung from, Ben pushed back. "You didn't have to sit there alone."

Her chin angled stubbornly at him, her lips pressing together in a tight line.

He wanted to shake her. "I did as you asked."

"You did." Her eyes grew round, not with fear, but with a deep sorrow he didn't think she knew was blazing at him, and something else. A response the desire eating away at him recognized.

She retreated. He advanced, his anger siphoning off, replaced by a different kind of frustration, until the goal post was at her back and she had nowhere else to go.

"There's no such thing as magic," he told her softly, believing it, but also knowing if it *was* real, it wasn't something he could help her find. Hadn't he learned that the hard way?

"There has to be," she whispered, her sweet breath kissing his chin.

Gently, so he didn't scare her away, he brushed the soft hair off her cheek, "We're water under the bridge."

"We are." Her eyes searched his, looking as baffled as he felt by the attraction sucking the air out of his lungs.

"Then, why do I want to do this?"

Before he could stop himself, Ben took her face in both

hands, and giving her time to say, no, slowly covered her inviting lips with his.

That's where caution ended. It wasn't just any kiss. Mountains leveled. The river rerouted itself around Rosewood. His heart pounded with unleashed desire to a primitive drumbeat in his ears.

Greedy hands fisted in his shirt, making him wish the barrier away. Raging hunger had him begging entrance into her lush mouth. When she gave in, he leaned her against the goal post, stepping between her legs. His hoodie slipped to the ground. He found her soft mounds and rubbed. His pants grew uncomfortably tight. There was no question about it. He wanted *her*. Now. Every which way possible.

Wanting to be completely buried in the welcoming warm of the woman tearing his logical, sensible plans to shreds, thoroughly shaken, he let her go and dragged in a ragged breath. "This time I won't apologize."

"God, I hope not. But, this is the end of it, right?"

Her breath came fast and furious, her chest rising and falling, the need plowing through his body making a laughing stock of the restraint he was attempting to enforce. It was all he could do not to go back for more.

Reason finally took the high road. "Yes."

She picked up his sweatshirt; held it out to him, her hand shaking slightly. "Good. I wanted to talk to you about the issue that came out today. It was very well received. I think we should work on a more comprehensive marketing plan. We can do better than distribute in Rosewood and the surrounding areas."

He took the garment from her, their fingers brushing. The zing of excitement that raced along his arm was mirrored in her desire-saturated eyes.

At least he wasn't the only one affected by the chemistry sparking between them.

Wrestling with his own arousal, Ben grabbed at the lifeline she offered. "I was thinking we could dedicate a column to a series of pieces on Portland, or Seattle. Readers would love a travel log about the local scene."

TWELVE

Monday morning came too quick for Syd. Ben was running late, or maybe he wasn't, because he hadn't said exactly when he would be there to go over the next issue of *The Gazette*.

She'd spent all weekend trying not to think about that earth-shattering kiss; assuring herself, it meant nothing to either of them. That the supernova lip-lock was just a natural expression of...loneliness between two consenting old friends.

That got her nowhere, except *thinking* about it. Again. And the feel of his hands molding her, promising a life-altering ride. Her skin heated.

Oh, for heaven's sake. She was a big girl. What was done was done. She didn't *need* a repeat performance.

Emerging from her room, Meredith held out a thin hand, interrupting Syd's dangerous reverie. "Come sit with me for a minute."

"What's going on?"

"I'll pack your medicines." Doc put his doctor's bag and a suitcase by the front door, then disappeared into the kitchen.

Syd frowned at his back as Meredith sank slowly to the couch. "What does he want with your medicines? Are you alright?"

Meredith shook her head. "I'm not dying, but the truth is,

I'm not getting better, either."

Syd sucked in a quick breath. When she went to question Meredith further, she was stopped by a shaky hand on her arm. "Doc has a plan, but that's not what I want to talk to you about. It bothers me that I'm the reason you didn't get to go to New York."

Syd squeezed her hand reassuringly. "Don't worry. Your stroke caused a little delay, but I'm still going."

A sad smile tugged on the corners of Meredith's mouth. "Don't get me wrong. I didn't *want* you to go, and still think you belong here, in Rosewood. I haven't changed my mind about that. It's just that all this drama wasn't the argument I planned to use."

Syd wished for the words that would make the other woman feel better.

"If nothing else, this stroke has made me realize something. There are a lot more days behind me than in front, and there's no time to waste." Meredith squared her shoulders. "So I've decided to commission a book on the history of Rosewood. Pictures and all the history you can dig up. It'll be my legacy to the town."

Meredith had never wasted a day in her life, as far as Syd could remember. She was about to protest when she caught on to her friend and mentor's implication. "What do you mean, all the history I can dig up?"

"I want you to take all the pictures you can, and write the book. I'll have my attorney draw up a contract."

A balloon of excitement filled in Syd's chest, but caution

got the upper hand. "I won't be here long enough to write a book."

Meredith rose as Doc came back into the room. "Doesn't matter. You can get started while you're waiting for that job of yours to come along."

The proposition sounded suspicious, but Syd didn't care. A chance to do something as interesting and challenging as a book? She stood with Meredith. An image of Ben's rugged face, grey eyes brimming with stormy passion, elbowed its way through her excitement. "I guess I can work on it in between working for Ben at *The Gazette*, and raising funds for the new library."

Meredith patted Syd's face, amusement bringing a sparkle to her tired eyes. "I have complete confidence that you can do it."

Doc grabbed the suitcase and put his bag under his arm. Syd raised a brow at the proprietary way he held Meredith's arm. "Where are you going?"

"To stay with Doc. His housekeeper's going to look after me and take me to my therapy sessions. It'll save him having to stop by every morning."

"But–" *that's why I'm here*, Syd struggled to say.

"I need you to feed Larry. His food is in the cupboard by the fridge. He also likes to go out in the mornings. And it wouldn't hurt *you* to go out on a date once in awhile."

"Don't you worry none. Alice will keep a close eye on Meredith," Doc said as he guided his patient out the door and to his waiting car.

Settled in the front seat after Doc fastened the seat belt around her, Meredith rolled down the window and waived her fingers at Syd.

She watched them drive away, then slowly closed the door, sinking a little breathless onto the couch. "Well. Okay."

What the heck just happened? Before she could sort it out, the doorbell peeled through the house. When she opened the door, it was the last person she was expecting to see.

Isabel flew past Ben, an agitated whirlwind in the guise of one clearly unhappy ten year old. She flopped on the couch; shoved her arms together across her chest.

Scowling, he followed his daughter. Dressed in jeans and a white dress shirt showing a sprinkle of dark chest hair at the vee of his neck, he was too yummy for words. It was all Syd could do to remember she'd barely recovered from the knee-buckling heat in his kiss. She didn't need to be wishing for more of the same.

"That's enough of this, young lady."

Ben's voice rumbled through her defenses like a tank on steroids. Isabel returned her father's scowl.

He stopped in front of Syd, his woodsy cologne taking over her senses. "We're having one of those days. She won't go to school."

He was clearly exasperated, but not as exasperated as she was by the sudden attack of an overwhelming urge to throw herself into his arms. She wasn't one of those ladies who needed saving she used to read about in the historical novels she'd snuck from her mother's beside table.

Fat tears welled in Isabel's eyes. "I don't want to go to school. You can't make me."

"What happened?"

Ben canted his head toward the kitchen side of the house, leading the way until he reached the French doors leading to the patio and garden.

Speaking in an undertone, he shoved his hands into his pockets. "We ran into Kevin on Saturday. He was mowing a neighbor's lawn. He said he'd come do ours yesterday, but he didn't show, and didn't call. Isabel is certain it's because of something she said."

"Which was?"

"She wouldn't tell me."

For a ten year old, friends were the most important measuring stick. Despite the fact that she should head for cover, and fast, a spike of sympathy robbed Syd of an easy escape route at Ben's obvious distress.

His frown deepened. "Do you know where Kevin lives? I could pick him up on the way to school and straighten out this whole mess."

Syd wanted to give the frustrated man the biggest hug. Papa Bear was determined to lumber into action and save his little girl's hurt feelings. "Isabel won't appreciate that."

His stormy eyes closed. "What can I do?"

Without considering the consequences, she covered his heart. He flattened his hand over her splayed fingers. The warmth of his touch heated her skin to fever pitch. When his eyes snapped open, they were the color of molten silver. Syd nearly drowned in them.

"Where's Meredith?" Isabel's hands were shoved in her pockets in perfect imitation of her dad's earlier stance. "She's not in her room."

She jerked her hand free. How in the world did she...the three of them...and her last days in Rosewood...get so wound together? It wasn't like they were the Three Musketeers or anything.

"She's gone to stay with Doc for awhile."

Ben leaned against the French door, the casual move hiding the heat in his expression. "So, what are you going to do?"

"I don't know. Babysit Larry, I'm told. Write a book. I have orders to go on a date." Syd flushed. She shrugged her shoulders. She hadn't meant to let *that* out of the bag.

When it seemed like he intended to pursue the subject, she shook her head. "Don't ask."

Determined to keep to the decision she'd made during the weekend, she switched her attention to Isabel. Ben Quincy was off limits. Permanently.

His delightful daughter wasn't, however. "So young lady, what's this about you not going to school?"

Isabel's liquid gaze dropped. "I don't like it there," she mumbled.

Syd struggled to keep her mind on the girl and off Ben, who was watching her, his handsome face revealing nothing. "I see."

He finally transferred his cooled-off gaze to Isabel. "So

you don't want to be a tutor anymore?"

"I guess." The child's chin wobbled. "I want to work at the paper with you."

It took every scrap of strength Syd possessed not to grab Isabel and offer comfort. The father, too, when the stern look in his eyes wavered.

"You have to go to school. That's the law, kiddo."

How he remained firm, Syd didn't know. It would have been impossible for her. Before she interfered where she wasn't wanted, she went looking for a glass of water.

Sipping the blessedly cool liquid, she watched the two of them. Ben was good at this. She, of course, had no experience being a parent. But her admiration for the man and what he was trying to do had been growing exponentially, until now all that admiration was about to tip the scales into something more. Something that would do a lot of damage to her heart when she left.

"The law's not fair. I want to be with you."

"I want you to be with me too, but what would you do at a newspaper? There's no jobs for a ten year old. You're not even old enough to get a work permit."

Syd slid on the slippery slope of not getting involved. Couldn't stop herself from falling right off the edge of the cliff. "I could use a junior reporter."

Their identical expressions, mixed with hope and disbelief, were comical, if it wasn't for the fact she'd stepped over a line she'd sworn to stay on her own side of.

"A junior reporter. Someone who reports... school

news...what's happening...what the students are doing."

When neither of them spoke, Syd swallowed hard. Maybe it wasn't such a good idea. She should have left well enough alone. The Quincy's could settle their problems without her feeble attempt to make things better.

Then Ben blinked, the quirk of his lips conveying gratitude as his heated gaze slid over her face, settling at last on her mouth, a caress as potent as the kiss she'd been working so hard to forget. "That's a great idea."

He shifted his attention to his daughter. Thank God.

If the giggle bubbling in her chest like a first time, in-love teenager came out, Syd was going to throw herself in Meredith's pond in the back yard. She was saved the trouble when Ben slung his arm around Isabel.

"Your first assignment will be to write an article on how to become a tutor."

Isabel's misery fled, her eyes growing round with excitement. "Awesome."

Ben grinned. Syd's heart was trapped.

He gave his daughter a quick squeeze. "But the same thing I told Kevin applies. You go to school every day, and maintain good grades. No complaints, alright?"

For a second, before she could catch herself and put her scrambling feet on firmer ground, Syd wished she was part of their family circle. It was laughable really, the temptation closing in on her; how she was growing attached to the gifted child. And, the man tearing through her defenses.

She'd given up the right to think of him as something

more a long time ago. The only problem was, she wanted him in the worst way, and not just between the sheets. This feeling overwhelming her good sense had nothing to do with their shared history, and everything to do with his sincere desire to do the right thing by his daughter.

Isabel extended her pinky. "Swear?"

Crap!

Father and daughter did the pinky swear, and snap, Syd was standing on a high wire, suspended between the life she was chasing and an old dream finding its way out of the dark cavern of her heart where she'd hidden it eons ago.

One thought chased her galloping heartbeat. With Meredith moving to Doc's place, there was nothing keeping her in Rosewood. If she found a babysitter for Larry – even though he was a mangy creature, how hard could that be – she'd be free to leave town anytime she wanted.

Except there was the book Meredith wanted her to do. And the fact that there was no job waiting on the horizon.

During her moment of hesitation, Ben moved in. Startled, she stared into his probing eyes. "Come to the school with us."

Her knees lost their strength. "Does Isabel want me to?"

Before his daughter could say ya or nay, his deep baritone crawled inside Syd, igniting a fire that ate away at her resistance. "*I* want you to."

~*~

At the school, once again Ben found himself sitting across the desk from Jenny Penhollow. She didn't find the idea of Isabel tutoring other students the least bit unlikely or objectionable. While the necessary paperwork to get his daughter started on her new adventure was being filled out, he began to wonder if the impossible was indeed possible?

In this alternate future, Isabel was happily settled in school, laughing, at the center of a flock...or was it gaggle...of girls. They were all best friends. Her band recital was awesome, her performance hands down better than all the other kids.

Sydney sat beside him during the show, her fingers laced with his, her sweet scent as potent as Isabel's success. The three of them were one happy family.

That's when the dream came to an screeching halt. Nothing had changed. Except, he couldn't get Sydney off his mind. Ten minutes didn't go by when he wasn't thinking of her; wondering what it would be like to strip her to her vanilla scented, soft skin and take thorough advantage of being her lover. Would she object and stop him? Or would she welcome him with open arms?

"Thanks Jenny. We'll come back on Wednesday to see if you have a student for Isabel. Is that okay with you, Ben?" Sydney looked at him expectantly.

He didn't dare meet her glorious topaz eyes. Not if he wanted to keep his wits about him. "Sure. Fine by me."

After Isabel skipped off to class, he gave himself one hell of a lecture all the way to the car.

They weren't a family. Sydney would be gone before they knew it, and he would be the one left to sweep up the pieces. Hopefully better than he had the last time.

But when they both reached for the passenger-side door handle, and their hands collided, fingers instinctively intertwining, he forgot every single, cautionary word of the pep talk. Searching the delicate face close enough to kiss, he found something he wasn't expecting. Sydney Marshall, once the love of his life, was as confused and...bothered as he was.

Everything turned upside down. He tugged her closer. This time, at least he knew what he was doing. It was an itch. One he'd forgotten she could bring on with her sassy look. But, he wasn't a randy teenager anymore. And when she left? He wouldn't feel nearly as empty as he had the last time.

He let his gaze drift to her half-opened lips, and whispered, "Come home with me."

~*~

Her breath stopped her throat. With a sudden jerk of her chin, Syd nodded. At the hot flair of desire that darkened the grey of his eyes, she let Ben ease her into the car; allowed his heat to envelope her as he reached across her lap to buckle the seat belt.

What was she doing? This was crazy. She couldn't possibly be considering doing *that*, could she?

But when he parked, pinned her with a look that had her going hot and cold all at once, and asked, "You sure?" she suddenly realized she'd been wanting to be with him this way for days.

She couldn't say, no, so she took the hand he offered and followed him into the house, every one of her senses coming alive and attuning to the man changing all the rules as she knew them. Maybe if she gave into the craving waking from its long sleep, just this once, then she could be done with it. And Ben. Finally close the door on their last disastrous parting.

He nudged her against the wooden door after closing and locking it. Taking command of her lips, he made short work of the buttons of her shirt.

She struggled to breath normally; to have the truth between them. "I'm leaving soon."

He eased the soft cotton off her shoulders, his lips leaving a trail of velvety awareness across her suddenly sensitized skin. "I know. I sent out three resumes for you this morning."

She pulled back. "You did what?"

The eyes that settled on her face were dark with arousal. He shrugged, a flush tinting the skin over his cheek bones. "You deserve to be happy."

Her anger totally annihilated, and intrigued more than she aught to be, she took his hand and drew him toward the dimly lit stairs. She already knew his bedroom was on the second floor. "Happy?"

He stopped her mid-way, their heated gazes level. Gently, he brushed the hair back from her face. His touch ignited a firestorm that took away what little breath she had left.

"You want every day packed full of excitement and adventure." He kissed her, nipping at her bottom lip, and backed her up a step. "You want to see the world. Explore every possibility life has to offer."

Sliding her arms around his neck, she drew him up

another step. Her hungry lips foraged where they would as she tangled her fingers in the thick strands of his hair. The low growl erupting from his throat was perfect reward.

He edged her to the next step. "You're funny, and brave."

Feeling like a bucket of cold water drenched her, Syd dropped her arms. "I'm not brave. I'm a coward."

Ben silenced her with a finger across her lips. "Don't argue with me, woman." He leaned in, bringing that seductive mouth close, but not close enough. "You're the bravest person I know."

Then he grabbed her, tossed her over his shoulder and took the rest of the stairs two at a time.

A sharp laugh bounced out of Syd. "Put me down, you crazy man."

He did. By tossing her onto the bed. His fingers a bit clumsy she noticed, he unbuttoned his shirt. "Get those clothes off, sexy girl. Wait. I'll take them off."

Faster than lightening, he shimmied out of his jeans and under-clothes.

Eyes closing at the sharp tumble of desire turning her inside-out at the sight of his incredible body, on the backside of her lids, like an old fashioned reel movie, Syd could see all the times Ben struggled to be a good father. How he'd taken Kevin under his wing. The way he fit into the town of Rosewood as if it was a glove made especially to fit him.

"We're friends?" That's what she'd missed the most while he was gone.

The bed eased under his weight. "Yes."

Grasping for some...she didn't know what exactly...sanity? She opened her eyes. "Being together...like this...won't change that?"

A gentle finger skimmed along her jaw leaving her defenseless in its wake. "We'll always be friends."

A friend with privileges. Was that what she wanted?

Everything changed. On a dime. At the Universe's capricious whim. She knew all about that. But, it was too late to stop what they'd started. She wanted Ben. Wanted him deep inside her, more than she wanted anything else at that moment.

"Promise."

"Pinky swear."

At the soft promise in his husky voice, she gave into the powerful emotions turning her inside out, and the man pushing her out of her safe, comfortable place. She'd deal with the fallout later.

As she skimmed out of her shirt and bra, hands tangled in their hurry to get rid of the rest of her clothes. Her back arched when his marauding lips found her breasts.

She gloried in the tongue and teeth that explored every inch of her throbbing body. At some point, she ended on top, and paid the charming man back for the lunacy he so cleverly orchestrated.

When he flipped her, knelt between her spayed knees to apply a condom, then entered her with a thrust that completely united them, time stood still, and it was a long time before sanity had the audacity to return.

THIRTEEN

After getting Isabel settled in the children section of the library, Ben hovered at the door, watching to make sure she was okay with him leaving.

When he'd suggested going to Library Night – an attempt to get kids to read that had been held at the Rosewood Library every Tuesday night for as long as Ben could remember – she'd sneered and shrugged carelessly. Then, after school, in a complete reversal, she'd announced she wanted to write a story for the paper about the event.

He suspected Isabel thought Kevin would be there, but the library didn't seem like a place where the boy would hang out, and he'd been a no show at *The Gazette*, like someone else he knew.

So there Isabel was, dressed in her pj's, like the other kids; black, he realized when she took off her sweatshirt, her hair tangled in a knot with a black bandana. A steno pad and pencil were gripped tightly with both hands.

When she looked around and saw he was still there, a scowl blossomed on her sweet face. She'd told him to go when they'd first arrived, but it'd felt too much like the last time you-know-who had ordered him to leave, and so his feet had remained rooted to the worn linoleum floor, refusing to move.

Isabel's scowl deepened. Ben held up his hands and

mouthed, *I'm going.*

As the door closed behind him, the crisp night air did wonders for clearing his head. He had three hours before he had to retrieve Isabel to run Sydney to ground. It was time to find out what was going on in the woman's pretty head.

He rounded the aging brick building where the library was squished in with City Hall. He could be honest...at least with himself. Discussing ideas with his co-chair for raising money to pay for the new library was the excuse he was using for hunting her down. The real reason – and he shouldn't be giving it a second thought – was he wanted to know what she'd meant by her parting words when she'd abruptly run off after spending an earth-shattering morning in his bed.

Nice? What the hell was that supposed to mean?

One minute they were bathing in a pretty impressive afterglow, his hands sliding over her supple back, on way to palming the lush curves of her tantalizing bottom.

The next she'd jumped out of the bed, grabbed her clothes off the floor, and hoping from foot to foot, shoved spectacular, long legs into her jeans – sans underwear by-the-way – giving him visions of pulling her back into the bed and continuing where they'd left off. Then she'd hastily pulled her shirt on, and was already at the door when his mush for brains snapped awake.

It wasn't out of line to ask – alright, so he'd demanded – where she was going. It was a reasonable question, after all. *That was nice, but I've...uh...got to get back to...work.*

Before he could stop her, show her how much better than

nice he could be, she was gone, her bare feet pounding on the stairs, the front door slamming in her hurry to leave.

Eyes narrowed, his temper simmered. *Nice?* Pfft.

He parked in front of Meredith's house, hoping the light shining from the windows meant Sydney was home. She wasn't answering his calls, and the only contact he'd had with the escape artist since that morning at his house, had been via email when she sent him updates on her progress.

They would get this straightened out right now. His hand stalled before thumbing the doorbell.

She'd run mighty fast. Again. And now she was in hiding. It was so out of character with what he'd learned of the woman since his return. The Sydney he'd gotten to know over the last few weeks took her licks on the chin. She didn't run and hide with her tail tucked between her legs. He was missing something.

He pinched the bridge of his nose. What did he expect from her? They'd made no promises, just scratched a mutual itch. Indulged in a bit of casual sex. Even though the sex itself had been mind-blowing, casual was all it could be.

He might be so attracted to the dratted woman he couldn't see straight, but the real truth was, he couldn't trust her, could he?

If all he had to worry about was himself, maybe he'd take the risk. But he had Isabel's already battered heart to consider and protect. The problem? He was scary afraid he'd never stopped loving Sydney Marshall.

Which was why he was standing on Meredith's doorstep.

To find out. He hit the doorbell. It chimed distantly through the house.

Impressions from their tumble between the sheets persisted in reshuffling; hammering at his renewed determination to keep things simple between them, sex or no sex, it didn't matter. Vivid pictures of how well they fit together. How wildly responsive she was to his seeking hands. And for the first time in years, how he hadn't felt quite so empty.

After his mistake with first Sydney, then Diana, he'd believed there was no woman out there who was his perfect match. Lately, he hadn't been willing to settle for less. And then–

Clearly Sydney wasn't that woman, except that when the world had shattered, buried completely in her warmth as he was, her arms and incredible legs holding him immobile in the moment, old feelings had begun to resurrect. A spark of hope ignited. For a nanosecond, he'd thought, just maybe, he could turn the clock back.

He shook his head. Experience had taught him better. A swift kick in the ass might straighten him out, but could it be possible, even remotely, making a home for Isabel in Rosewood wasn't all he wanted anymore?

Shaken, he stepped off the porch, half turned to return to his car. Behind him, the door opened. "Ben?"

He spun around, first glance taking in the cautious downturn of Sydney's mouth; the wariness spilling from her tired brown eyes. All that had passed between them, including their time together yesterday morning – limbs, straining bodies, and mutual need all tangled – stretched taunt between them.

"I...uh...thought we should–" his mind jumped to the crowded library when he'd left Isabel. "–brainstorm ideas to fund-raise for the new library."

Suddenly, having that discussion at Meredith's empty house, where he could so easily forget how unwise it would be to initiate a repeat performance by pulling Sydney into a crushing embrace and cover those kissable lips with his own rampant hunger; demonstrating just how *nice* he could be; it didn't seem like such a good idea.

The very last thing he needed was to get involved with Sydney Marshall all over again, and be dealt a second hand of heartbreak.

"Have you eaten? Do you want to go to the Ranger Saloon for a burger?"

~*~

Having an affair with Benjamin Quincy was not what Syd had envisioned all those years ago when they were in high school. Her feelings back then had been solely about the long haul.

While it had been rocking spectacular, having sex with the man studying her from the other side of the table had also been a big mistake. Going to dinner with him was a bigger mistake.

Sex? Is that what they call it these days? The man is sexy enough to grace the cover of GQ. A couple of hours making wild monkey love, and he manages to rearranged your whole world. Just sex? Paleese.

He doesn't love me. He never did, Syd argued with the she-devil sneering from the center of the whirling tornado making it difficult to breath. *If he did, he wouldn't have gone right out and gotten himself a wife and child.*

The echo of a snicker rattled in her chest.

The morning spent in Ben's bed had changed everything. And nothing.

She plastered studied indifference on her face. So what if she didn't trust herself to take the right road where the bothersome man was concerned. Once before she'd made a choice based on longing, and at her dying father's urging. It was the wrong decision and the cost had been those last precious moments of her father's life.

"Kevin hasn't been in school since Friday."

Her thoughts kept whirling, but she stopped making circles on the dark wood of the table with her beer glass. "How do you know that?"

"Isabel."

Why am I not Isabel's mother? She knew why.

"He hasn't come to *The Gazette* after school, either."

Sudden apprehension splashed cold water on her brooding. She frowned at Ben. "We could go to his house. Check on him."

His jaw hardened. "If he's not at school tomorrow morning, we'll do that, and if there's been trouble we'll go to the Sheriff's."

Here was a man determined to do everything he could to protect his family. Even take care of a boy who wasn't his to protect. Warmth filled Syd's chest, then iced over as quickly as it'd grown.

For good reason, she'd sacrificed her chance to be the one Ben turned to. She hadn't wanted him to get buried with her in Rosewood; should have figured out sooner the little town was exactly where he belonged.

Rosewood didn't need her, but the small community definitely needed Ben. Longing so deep, and so illogical it hurt, sprang from the darkest part of her heart. She straightened; pressed her lips together. Now was not the time to be questioning the decisions she'd made...or would make in the future.

With the lights of the bar burning low, murmurings of a multitude of conversations wrapped her with Ben in an inviting intimacy that nearly chased her back to the solitude of Meredith's house. Alone.

Her heart suddenly stopped beating. She didn't want to be alone. Like it or not, for better or worse, she was temporarily embroiled in more than a casual way with Ben and his daughter. The girl was prone to making wrong choices. Like Syd was. Who wouldn't fall in love with the child, and the father hell bent on giving her the perfect life?

Except she wasn't *in love* with Ben. She was only drawn to him because he fit so completely into the meandering rhythm of their hometown, and it'd turned out she was leaving *The Gazette* in good hands.

If things were different – but they were ships passing in the proverbial night, their only purpose in being together to keep a faltering town icon from going under, and to raise money for Rosewood's much needed library.

You have a second chance, the she-devil whispered to Syd's dismay.

It was too tempting to throw caution to the wind; to take the strong hand resting on the table and give in to the yearning pulsing through her like a train chugging down the tracks to its destination.

In desperation, she shoved her hands beneath her legs and sat on them.

Damn. Damn. Damn. She blurted, "What about starting a game night to launch our fund raising efforts. We could hold it at the community center."

Ben nodded, "Not a bad idea."

He'd somehow managed to find her foot under the table and trapped her shoe between his boots. At her frown, a sexy grin spread across his rugged face.

Thank goodness the barmaid brought their food. She jerked her foot out of reach, firmly steering her attention away from the smugly smiling man sitting across from her, concentrating instead on the soup and club sandwich she'd ordered.

~*~

After Sydney had freed her foot from between his boots, the stunned look on her pretty face had kept Ben on the edge of his seat for the rest of the meal, which had been spent in tantalizing conversation, talking around what was really on their minds, as they came up with several ways to earn money for the cause.

He'd taken her back to Meredith's, kept his hands to himself, watched from the car until she got to the house. Before closing the door she'd cast a look over her shoulder, and he'd glimpsed the same hunger he'd seen in her beautiful eyes periodically throughout dinner.

It had taken all his considerable will power not to follow and knock on her door. With Isabel waiting for him to come get her, the timing was lousy.

But there wasn't a good time to figured out what he honestly wanted from Sydney. And by the time Isabel stomped into the kitchen the next morning, he'd convinced himself, this aching need to spend every moment, waking, or not, with Sydney was his libido clamoring for simple satisfaction.

Except nothing about his relationship – or lack of one – with Sydney Marshall was simple. And neither was the rest of his life.

When he'd pick Isabel up from the library, she'd been too quiet. And now they were back to black, from head to toe, accompanied by black biker boots he hadn't seen before and a black cap hiding her pretty blonde hair.

"Does your mother actually allow you to wear that...stuff?"

He winced. He didn't know what was worse. His demented need to be with a woman who'd already given him a swift kick in the teeth, or the trying to be a good parent to angry child glaring at him.

Hanging onto his gaze defiantly, Isabel shoved a sheaf of papers into his hands. Black circled her eyes; lashes clumped with ill-applied mascara. Where in the double hockey sticks had she gotten the stuff?

He pointed to the bathroom. "Makeup off."

Her chin jerked up. "But, Dad–"

"Now, if you don't want to be grounded for life."

She spun on her heel with a stomp, but headed for the downstairs bathroom. When the water gushed on, he looked at the papers she'd given him; quickly read through the articles she'd written.

He started toward the bathroom as she emerged with a clean face. "These are good."

One shoulder slipped glumly up and down. "Whatever."

She'd retreated. On a resigned sigh, Ben tried again. He might be a clueless man when it came to the women in his life, but he wasn't about to let his daughter be miserable because of his ineptitude. "Really, baby. These are very good."

Tears filled her eyes. "Maybe."

Ben squatted so they were on the same eye level. "I wouldn't lie to you."

She dropped her gaze to her feet. "I know."

Carefully Ben removed the cap and placed a kiss on her forehead. "You look much better without this."

She eyed him dubiously.

He held his hands in mock surrender. "I swear."

She finally allowed a small, trembling smile.

"There's my girl. Now, how about we get you to school?"

With an over-exaggerated sigh, she grabbed her book bag and headed for the car. The conversation on the way was mostly one-sided, but hey, at least she was only half-Goth this morning, rather than the full meal deal. He had to take his miracles where he could get them.

Sydney waited for them at the front of the school, and it wasn't feelings of a boss meeting with his employee washing over him at the sight of her. He slowed his steps to prove he could withstand the impossible attraction, waiting until he got close to ask, "Did Kevin make it?"

Sydney shoved her hands in her back pockets. "I haven't seen him yet."

Ben tried not to notice how great she looked in the snug fitting denim.

"You're looking for Kevin? I know where his first class is."

Sydney took Isabel's hand. "Show us."

He followed at a safe distance and hoped the churning in his stomach at the two of them, heads bent close together, wasn't going to last all day. They found Kevin outside his Home Room, rushing to get there before the tardy bell rang.

He skidded to a stop when he saw them. Panic flitted across his face, replaced quickly by cocky disdain.

Ben felt sorry for his daughter, but suddenly proud too, when she stared Kevin down.

"What happened to your arm?" Sydney asked in the awkward silence, reaching for Kevin's chin to better see the scratches carved into his skin. It wasn't until then Ben realized the boy's arm was in a sling.

Kevin backed away from Sydney. "I was cleaning the gutters and fell off the roof."

Fear flickered momentarily in his eyes. A lie then, but why?

Ben started to question him further, but Sydney beat him to the punch, insisting softly, "Your reading lesson is third period. We'll meet in the library."

Kevin hesitated, then winced as he shrugged. "Yes, ma'am."

"Don't be late."

He hurried into his classroom, and they retraced their steps, stopping in front of Isabel's room.

Isabel threw herself into Sydney's arms. "Thanks."

Wonder spread across Sydney's face in a pink flush as her arms circle Isabel and they both held on tight. Ben shook his head. He was sinking fast.

"I'll talk to Ms. Penhollow about getting you out of class so you can come to the library too. Meet me there during second period and we'll go over the things you need to know about tutoring your first student."

"Awesome." Isabel smiled for the first time that morning, and bounced into class.

Ben grasped for the reality slipping through his fingers. If he wasn't careful, and the pressure in his chest wasn't a heart attack but the one thing he couldn't trust Sydney to return in kind, all the woman who'd just made everything right for his little girl had to do was crook her little finger, and he'd be hers for the taking.

FOURTEEN

This wasn't happening. Again.

Then why was the thought of dragging Ben back to bed sneaking up on her with more and more regularity. If she didn't know better, she'd say she was jonesing for her ex's mind-blowing touch, and wasn't that just not the truth at all.

She winced. What they'd done should be illegal, but Ben had managed to touch her in a way she hadn't expected. Completely losing herself in his capable arms scared her, and made the decisions she had to make more difficult; a complication she couldn't allow.

What she needed...well never mind that. What she didn't need was this twisty...knotted...road that kept her from the goal she'd spent every waking breath working toward. That is until Ben returned.

The image of him naked, his strong legs tangled with hers wouldn't go away, no matter how hard she tried to keep it at bay. She pressed her lips together, deleting the thought as though it was a picture on her monitor she couldn't bear to keep staring at.

First to arrive at the community center where she was supposed to meet Ben and Shelly Pearman, the Director of the center, she pulled into a parking spot. Taking advantage of the moment to catch her breath, she shifted her thoughts into more organized lines instead of the convoluted mess muddying the path she'd already laid out ahead of her.

Restless, she climbed out of her Volkswagen, paced the length of the white building, arms wrapped around her middle, and found herself staring at the big oak at the end of the center. It was the oldest tree in town. Some estimated one-hundred and fifty years, but no one really knew.

Just like she didn't know for certain if it would actually, metaphorically speaking anyway, kill her if she turned out to be one of those people who never went further than a three hundred mile radius from her hometown.

And for the sake of argument, what if she ended up – through no fault of her own – staying in Rosewood? She'd probably survive, and life would go on.

But deep inside, she was deathly afraid if she spent the rest of her life doing nothing more than she was doing right this minute, working for a small town newspaper, struggling to raise funds to build a new library, tutoring in her spare time...all meaningful pursuits, she would never discover the adventurous woman hiding inside.

Ever since Ben had returned, things were different. *She* was different. He had her longing twisting back on itself, like hairpin curves, the way it hadn't in years.

She was seeing the town through his eyes, him though his daughter's eyes. Thinking maybe, there was still a connection between her and the man who was once – a very long time ago – the light of her world.

It was wrong. All wrong. If she went with her gut

feelings where Ben Quincy was concerned; if she followed the instincts that kept insisting maybe she could have more than a flashy lifestyle that took her around the globe, she might once again make the wrong decision.

If she did that, it *would* kill her.

Under a cooling sun hanging low in the clear fall sky, she kicked at the ground. It would be a shame, was all she was saying. She was a travel writer. She wanted to travel.

"Hey. Are you alright?"

Syd spun at the rumble of his voice. The concern swirling in his grey eyes, flipped her stomach over.

Or, you could take the risk; find redemption after all this time; and start the greatest adventure of your life.

Her palms broke out in a sweat. Advice like that she could live without. "I'm fine."

The concern lingered. She saw the question gather in the stormy depths; held up her hand to stop his next question. "No job yet."

Shelly parked next to Ben's Camaro.

Syd headed for the entrance to the center. "Any word on the grant request?"

Ben shoved his hands in his pockets, staying close, his shoulder occasionally brushing hers. So much for clear, uncomplicated thinking.

"I talked to my resource at the Small Business Department, and he said, if we're lucky, it could take three months. If we're not so lucky, six."

She would be long gone by then.

"Hi Sydney, how's it going?" Shelly was an efficient, willowy redhead with the skin and temperament to match. She also loved her job as Director of the Community Center. They'd all known each other since grade school. "Ben, I heard you were back in town. Bought *The Gazette?*"

Shelly unlocked the door. Ben's smile was ultra-quick as he ushered Syd into the building. The flair of jealousy mingling with her confusion surprised her. Ben wasn't hers. Not in that way.

"Yup." He leaned around her to shake Shelly's hand, taking up space, chased her breath away. "It's nice to see you. Thanks for letting us take a look."

As soon as the door was pushed opened, Syd dashed in. The heat of Ben's body warming her from head to toe was just what she was trying to avoid.

She wandered around the open space while trying not to listen to Ben catch up with their old...well not so old...school mate. Shelly wasn't really *the other woman.*

"Hey Syd, did you hear someone bought the old theater?"

"Who?"

"No clue." Shelly gave them a jaunty wave. "Lock the door when you're done. And let me know what dates you want reserved."

When the door closed behind Shelly, Ben shot Syd a quizzical look. "This will do nicely for game night, don't you think?"

She hung back as he meandered around the open room. Large windows on two walls let in plenty of light. And suddenly, she realized, she liked his company. Enjoyed *him*.

Her she-devil snickered. She had to agree. In his jeans, Ben Quincy was a hot toddy. That much had not changed.

"How many tables do you think we can fit in here?"

She joined him at the head of the room. "Since we have to get the word out, and it'll take a couple of months to build up attendance, we can start with ten."

Hands perched low on his hips, he slowly paced to the center of the room. "We can have board games, Scrabble, checkers, chess, but what about a couple of computers for games, and maybe a Wii. Also, we'll need games for the kids, so families can participate. Maybe we could have a quilt auction, too?"

Syd loved the way his mind worked, how he circled a problem, then dove straight in. Why in the world was she considering depriving herself?

"Where's Isabel?" she asked, more than a little stunned at the direction her sudden desire to be with him was dragging her.

He started back across the room. "With Meredith."

"Did she tell you who she tutored today?"

"Yes. Kevin's little brother, Dillon."

"That's serendipitous, wouldn't you say?"

Dark brows shot up. "Only girls believe in that stuff."

She laughed at his skepticism. Feeling on firmer ground as he sauntered toward her, his lazy, confident stride doing mean things to her self-control, she came to a decision.

Since it looked like she was going to be cooling her heels

in Rosewood for the time being, she might as well throw herself wholeheartedly into raising funds for the new library. It was a worthy cause, and something she believed in.

While she was at it, it was also as good a time as any to get started on the book Meredith had commissioned. She had a ton of pictures in a large box she'd taken of the town and surrounding community over the years.

All this business had the added benefit of keeping her mind off the larger-than-life man baring down on her as though he had more on his mind than raising money for a good cause. Spinning on her heel, Syd led the charge out of the community center. "With some good advertizing, we can have the first event two weeks from tonight."

"Let's do it then." He locked the door as she bolted down the porch steps.

Her pulse jumped. She was pretty sure he hadn't meant that the way it sounded. But when she spun to face him, her breath locked in her chest. "I'll let Shelly know."

More than a little mischief sparkled in the grey eyes watching her. In fact the look shining there bordered on hot and steamy.

Syd couldn't help it. Her resistance crumbling as though it was made from the weakest mortar, her body responded without permission, sending out it's own signals. Suddenly tired of fighting the tension between them – actually a little excited to be back in the game – she backed toward her car, beckoning him with a flick of her fingers.

A grin spread across his handsome face as he followed,

catching up with her before she reached her Volkswagen. Long, strong fingers threaded through her hair. Chills of anticipation skimmed her flushed skin. The kiss he gave her was pure sinful. It made the sun shine brighter, and hotter. It moved planets out of their orbits. Then shifted everything Syd knew about herself.

Leaving? If she wasn't careful, if she gave into this...this...attraction; if she let her heart get involved...walking away was going to be near impossible.

Unfortunately the stern warning did not stop her from following Ben home.

~*~

Saturday morning an exuberant bounce on the bed from his child woke Ben from a sound sleep infused with x-rated dreams involving a certain woman. He checked the pillow beside him. She wasn't physically in his bed.

The sigh that slipped out was equally mixed with regret and relief. He wasn't ready to explain to Isabel what he was doing with Sydney. Hell, he wasn't sure he knew what he was doing with her. And he needed time to sort out his feelings, and this seemingly unquenchable need to touch her; be near her every moment he could.

Spending so much time with Sydney, stealing time when Isabel wasn't in the house, it wasn't smart. When she left it was going to hurt like a son-of-a-gun. At least that part he had experience with.

Ultimately, a couple of hot nights in the sack with the lady taking over his restless dreams, was all he was going to get. Someday, he might want to marry again; and he definitely wanted more children. Sydney wasn't the woman who would share that future. Was she?

"Dad! Wake up! Ms. Chartres says we have to get out to the estate sale early to get the best deals."

That was another thing. After spending the day with Sydney, and delivering fliers to local businesses for game night, he'd left a quiet Kevin cleaning the press room, while he went to get Isabel from school.

When he'd located her, she'd dragged him to a meeting at the old theater on the school grounds. It seemed she'd turned in her sax for a gig in community theater, and was all agog for him to meet the new director.

Belle Chartres was a well preserved octogenarian, who – as the scuttlebutt went – had spent most of her life on the New York stage. Long, thick white hair was piled on her head in what looked like a tangled knot. There was an energy in her step, every teenager in town must envy.

Ben certainly did. He needed that kind of energy to keep up with his daughter, and at the same time figure out what to do about Sydney and the fact that she was fast becoming more important to him than a casual affair should be.

"Da-ad. Get up!"

Ben groaned, rubbed at his eyes with the pads of his fingers, and shoved one leg out from beneath the covers. "I'm coming."

Damn it, he was a sucker for a beautiful woman, which is why Ms. Chartres had taken one look at him and seen sap written across his forehead. Suspicious of the sassy twinkle in the elegant woman's brown eyes, he'd almost missed Isabel's announcement.

She didn't want to perform on stage. No. She wanted to do costumes. And for the first time since bringing his daughter to the quaint town of his childhood, she was happy. Genuinely, smiling-ear-to-ear happy. How could he say no to anything she asked of him?

Before he knew it, he'd been drafted into taking Isabel to an estate sale on Edgewater, where they were to meet with Ms. Chartres and her assistant, and look for costumes suitable – her words, not his – for the upcoming production of the newly established Rosewood Performing Arts Group...a modern day version of *Pride And Prejudice.*

Isabel skipped out of the room, but was barely gone a few seconds before she poked her head back in. "Can Sydney go with us?"

"Uh...sure. But she's probably busy."

"Can I call her?"

He sat on the side of the bed; scrubbed his face. "I guess."

An hour later, Ben parked in the circular drive of the estate. Past the imposing mansion was a spectacular view of Rosewood. If he were a bird, he could fly off the cliff at the back of the magnificent house, wing over the Clackamas River straight into Main Street.

A few cars down from where he'd parked was Sydney's red Bug. Unwise anticipation had him looking to see if he could find her.

"Dad, we're late!" Isabel jumped out of the car.

Was it too late to see if what they'd started in high school was stronger than the wrong turns they'd taken in the intervening years? It was a big gamble, what he was contemplating. And Ben didn't have the slightest idea how to bridge the past into their present.

Wondering if he'd turned left onto Crazy Street, he wasn't far behind his excited daughter when she stopped with a skip and a hop in front of the very woman he was seriously considering turning in his sanity for.

Isabel lit up like a bright light coming on at dusk. She clung to Sydney's outstretched hand, skipping in a circle around the laughing woman making permanent inroads into his life.

It was the end of September, but the sun overhead was strong and warm, and it spun gold threads in Sydney's unruly hair. Her camera swung from one shoulder. Favorite jeans hugged her curvy hips and long legs. A ruffled short-sleeve blouse in varying shades of browns and oranges, swirled gracefully as she turned with Isabel. The well worn cowboy boots on her feet tromped their way right to the door of his heart.

Did he dare open it and invite this gorgeous, sweet woman in? It was too late. The door was wide open, and she was already settling in.

The sound of Sydney's delighted laughter drew him closer still. She let go of Isabel; snapped pictures of his daughter doing a exuberant dance.

The camera swung in his direction. She went still. A click took the place of her laughter. She lowered the Canon, smiling self-consciously. "Hi."

"Hi yourself."

She gestured toward the house. "I'm taking pictures for Meredith's book."

He couldn't help himself. He had to touch her; closed the distance to lay claim to the small of her back as he herded the woman and child into the house. "You're not planning to include that last one, I hope."

A saucy grin spread across her face, crinkling the edges of her stunning eyes. "We'll see."

He broke free of her spell, smoothed the top of Isabel's head. "So, what are we looking for?"

"Old fashioned dresses. And men's clothes, too."

"Alright. Let's take a look."

They followed a stream of curious buyers and sightseers into the mansion. A woman dressed in business black handed out maps, then directed them to follow a designated path past furniture marked with unobtrusive tags.

Sydney snapped pictures. Ben glanced at the map. "It says the clothing is located upstairs in the bedrooms."

On the second floor, the rooms were filled with racks and racks of old clothes. Ben hung back and watched while his girls – that had a nice ring to it – scavenged like true shoppers, looking over every item, discussing its merits, occasionally finding a fancy dress or men's trousers they couldn't put back. Those they pushed into his arms.

Watching them like that, it stunned Ben how much alike they were, his daughter and the woman who wasn't her bio-mother. Their heads bent close, the entire time their excited voices intermingled as though they'd been co-conspirators every day of Isabel's life.

He frowned as he followed the lure of their chatter into the next room. There they found the actress, who warmly wrapped bejeweled arms around Isabel and then introduce herself to Sydney.

As though it had a mind of its own, Sydney's camera came up. Ben smiled when she hesitated at the last moment. "Do you mind if I take your picture?"

"Of course not, dear." Ms. Chartres posed majestically for a few photos, then caught sight of him loitering in the background, enjoying the show. "Mr. Quincy, let's see what you have."

She took the clothes from him. He laughed. He couldn't help it. Being there with Sydney and Isabel, joining them in the fun of finding costumes for a play, being included in their adventure, it felt like he was suddenly living a dream he never knew he had. Spending the day in the company of his daughter and the woman he loved.

He went still. That was right. He was in love with the one woman who had the power to break his heart or make him so happy, he could fly without wings.

She'd already broken his heart once. Was he willing to risk that pain a second time?

She looked his way, her face alight with pleasure. When

her gaze locked with his, her smile softened into sweet longing. After spending the last month with her, he was beginning to believe in the magic she was seeking. A lock opened on his heart and there was no going back.

Hell yes! He was more than willing to take the risk.

FIFTEEN

*I*sabel went off with Belle Chartres, leaving Syd alone amongst the growing crowd with Ben. Butterflies fluttered in her stomach, which was silly really. Those butterflies had migrated a long time ago.

Something stirred in the stormy depths of his eyes. Something she was afraid to acknowledge. He held out a hand. "There's a balcony right through those doors. Let's check out the view."

She cautiously placed her hand in his. Strong fingers closed around hers, the warmth of his palm sending a shiver along her arm to settle around the bastion of her heart. The look in his eyes asked questions she didn't want to answer as he pulled her out onto the balcony.

When the tall, glass doors closed behind them, they had the balcony all to themselves. The view from the back of the house overlooked a luscious, well kept formal garden, making Syd think of a fairy tale. The scent of late blooming flowers turned the moment into a surreal cocoon she couldn't find the strength to break out of.

Ben cupped her face, slowly drawing her in for a kiss that reached all the way to her toes. Their tongues mated. His hands skimmed her back bringing her closer. Need, deep and irrefutable, took control.

"Do you believe in second chances?" he whispered when he finally broke off their kiss.

Syd's sluggish brain was slow to beat off the passion he'd stirred. "Second chances?"

She shook her head. He'd brought her out to see the view from the balcony. Instead she could see clear into his heart to a place she couldn't go. She pushed on his chest until he let her go.

"There are no second chances."

He watched her steadily. "I think there could be if we wanted one."

She edged back from the seductive future he dangled. "Are you saying you want to try?"

He followed her retreat across the balcony. "I'm saying I want more than a few nights between the sheets."

"But you don't love me."

He reached for her. She evaded the touch that would scramble her already fried thoughts.

He hesitated, his brows pulling together in a fierce frown. "I *do* love you."

"How?" Her back literally to the wall, she blurted. "I can't be with you."

He stopped a mere foot away. The lips she'd taken such pleasure in kissing pressed into a thin, harsh line. "Why?"

"I was there."

Confusion darkened his eyes. "Where?"

"At the University." At his blank look, she sucked in a breath. "In Chicago."

"When?"

Goaded, it all spewed out. "Four months after you left, my father talked me into going to Chicago to try and patch things up between us; to see if we could have a *second chance.*" It took what remaining strength she had not to sneer at the empty words. "When I got there, I was told I could find you in Family Housing."

The memory returned as clear as the day she'd stood across the street from the Student Residence building. Syd pressed her fingers to her trembling mouth. She'd been just in time to see Ben emerge, his arm wrapped around the shoulders of a tall, willowy woman who leaned heavily into his side.

"You came out with another girl." She couldn't breath. "You'd already moved on. I figure it was Isabel's mother. Now that I do the math, she was already pregnant, wasn't she?"

Ben had gone pale, his grey eyes deep wells of dark pain. He nodded. "I'm sorry."

Her broken laugh was the sound of glass shattering. "That's not the worst part. While I was there, desperate to get you back? My dad died. When I got home, he was gone. I'd wasted the last precious moments of his life chasing after a second chance that didn't exist."

He reached for her. She cringed against the wall. His arm dropped to his side, hands balling into fists. "God, Syd. I am so sorry. How will you ever forgive me?"

She drew in a shaky breath and stiffened her spine so she stood as tall as possible. Lifting her chin, she stared into his turbulent eyes and finally stopped running from the truth. "It's not you I have to forgive."

On that unchangeable fact, she walked around him, her head held high, and left Ben there, to his balcony, the noonday sun, and a daughter that wasn't hers, no matter how much Syd wanted her to be.

~*~

By Wednesday Ben figured he'd had enough. All he wanted was to talk to Sydney and figure out how to help the obstinate woman, because God help him, he was so in love with her it hurt to see her suffer for his dumb mistake.

Leaving his empty pop bottle on his desk, he snatched up his keys and after hanging a *Be right back* sign on the door, headed out to get Isabel.

He couldn't turn back the clock, wouldn't trade his daughter for anything or anyone in the world, but he wanted that second chance Sydney didn't believe in.

It wasn't going to happen if he couldn't get her to stop avoiding him like the plague. She was working from Meredith's. The emails she sent advising him of her progress with Game Night were polite. When he did get her to answer her cell, she was careful to keep miles between them.

Yesterday, she'd literally put one-hundred, twenty miles between them, leaving early in the morning before he could stop her, or suggest he go along, driving two and a half hours to a little ghost town in northeastern Oregon.

The email she'd sent at four in the morning said she was going to take pictures for an article she was planning for *The*

Gazette, but he suspected the real reason was to distance herself from him and their argument – if it could be called that – on Saturday. The good news was she planned to be back in time for the junior varsity game at six.

He stopped in front of the school and opened the car door for Isabel.

"Dad, can we take Dillon home?"

He remembered they'd had a tutoring session today. "Sure."

Dillon got in the back, but other than giving directions to his house, the boy remained silent. Ben frowned, drawn out of his own problems.

Isabel was awfully quite too. He glanced in her direction. "So, how was school today."

"Okay." She stared out the window.

Ben gave it another shot. "When do you work on the play again?"

"Tomorrow after school."

"We're still on for the game tonight, right?"

She looked briefly over her shoulder at their passenger, her mind miles away, and nodded.

He stopped at the curb in front of the house Dillon indicated. The boy jumped out. Without a word or glance back, he scuffed his feet up the walk, carefully closing the front door of the worn-looking house behind him.

Ben had only seen the kid from a distance, so he didn't know if the subdued behavior was normal or not. "Is something wrong?"

Isabel stared at the door, perhaps waiting for Kevin to come out. "It's a secret."

"I see."

She was quiet for the time it took to drive to *The Gazette.* He removed the sign from the door, ushering her in ahead of him. When she'd shrugged off her backpack, and pulled out her books to do her homework at the receptionist's desk – a position he needed to fill, but hadn't yet – a frown pulled her delicately drawn brows together.

Ben leaned on the edge of the desk. "What's the matter, baby?"

Her eyes stayed glued to her school book. "It's wrong, isn't it, for a dad to hurt his kid?"

Moving aside a copy of the last edition of the *Rosewood Gazette* he'd left there earlier, he settled more comfortably on the desk. "Yes. It is. No dad wants to hurt his children."

"Kevin's dad does."

"What happened? It's okay. I won't tell anyone," Ben reassured her gently, hoping the sick feeling in his stomach had no grounds to turn into burning anger; hoping that he would be able to keep that promise.

"Pinky swear?"

He wrapped his pinky around hers. When she finally looked at him, big, fatty tears rolled silently down her cheeks. Ben wanted to grab her and hold on tight, but he was afraid in his attempt to protect her from the ugly truth, he would crush her.

"Dillon said his dad beats on Kevin all the time. Then

yesterday, he started hitting Mrs. Newman, and Kevin got really mad, and beat up his dad."

Ben gave in to his instinct to hold onto Isabel and never let go. "What happened then?"

"Mr. Newman is gone. Kevin made him leave."

"Is Kevin hurt?"

"Dillon says he's okay, but he wasn't at school today."

He cradled Isabel's face in his hands, gently tilting her head until her swimming eyes were locked onto his. "We'll check on him at the game tonight. If he's not there, we'll go to his house and make sure he's alright. Okay?"

Isabel nodded, swiped the tears from her face with the back of her hand, and eased back into the desk chair as she opened her book. Ben gave her a swift hug.

"I'll be in the office if you need me."

His foot was on the first rung when she stopped him. "Dad?"

"What, baby?"

"I'm glad we moved here."

He was glad Kevin was unharmed. "Me, too."

He started up the stairs, but she stopped him again. "Are you going to marry Miss Sydney?"

And out of the mouth of his baby came the million dollar question.

~*~

Syd clutched her camera to her chest. She'd driven out to Shaniko to do her Clare Marsh thing. And to think. Or more like, to avoid scrutinizing too closely the bubble of excitement rising like a fireball of a new day inside her chest. But her mind never strayed far from Ben and how he had her wondering if things between them could turn out different this time, if she had the courage to take that first step.

The churning in her stomach that had gotten worse as the day progressed was why she was standing on the doorstep of her mother's new condo. First she'd gone to the house on Maple Street where she'd spent her early years, but everything there was packed in boxes, leaving an eerie silence and a vague sense that the family who had lived there was long gone. It'd felt like she was losing her dad all over again; her childhood dying with him one more time.

As she'd wandered through the house seeing herself as a little girl Isabel's age in every room, it'd hit her with the force of a sledge hammer. Lauren was lightening her life. Starting over.

For the first time in longer than Syd could remember, lonely for her mother's practical advise, she'd locked up the memories along with the door, and drove the short distance to Lauren's new place. Hand raised to knock, she frowned at the Sheriff's cruiser parked next to her mother's silver Tundra.

What was the Sheriff doing here?

The door opened. Her mother's laughter floated out with the elder Marshall's favorite lavender scent.

So, not arrested on embezzlement charges. Not that she would ever believe Lauren capable of committing any crime, much less stealing the library's money.

Busy flirting with whoever was still in the house, her

mother practically ran Syd over, catching herself at the last moment. That's when it hit. She hadn't seen her mother looking this happy since before her father's diagnosis. Lauren's streaked blonde hair hung loose to her shoulders. A tint of red spreading across her cheekbones, she pushed extra long bangs to the side of new, black wire-rim glasses.

Dressed head to toe in dark grey, slender fashionable pants clinging to her still remarkable figure, blazer to match covering a soft silk tank, the woman staring at her, apparently at a rare loss for words, was not the unadventurous mother who's only interest in clothes while Syd was young was that they be functional.

"Um...hi."

Her mom recovered quickly, leaning forward to place a kiss on her cheek. "Hi, sweetie."

Okay, what have you done with my mother?

A man in uniform stepped out of the house. The Sheriff belonging to the cruiser behind her, no doubt. He stopped close to Lauren's back as though he had the right to hover protectively.

Her mother angled a shoulder toward the man. "Syd, this is Sheriff Ethan Ford. He's investigating the library fund embezzlement."

Sheriff Ford was tall, greying at the temples of his military cut hair, built to impress a woman, even at his age – which Syd guessed was close to her mother's – and he was charming, if the amused twinkle in his forest green eyes as he stuck his hand out was anything to go by. "Nice to meet you."

Syd let her gaze swing between the two. His grip was polite, but strong. "Nice to meet you, too, Sheriff." *I think.*

She stared at her mom. The blush climbing Lauren's cheeks deepened. "He's...uh...helping me move some things into the condo."

Heading back down the sidewalk, she swallowed hard. *Oh my god! My mom had a boyfriend!*

Her mother followed, a frown marring her previous happiness as the Sheriff locked and closed the door. "Is something wrong?"

"No. No. Of course not." Lauren gave her that look. The one Syd recognized well from her childhood when her parent knew she was lying. She headed for her Volkswagen. "I can see you're busy."

"Hold it right there, Miss."

Syd stopped, looked at the sky, reluctantly obeying. It'd been a mistake to come.

"I'll wait by the car." His amusement gone, Sheriff Ford nodded briefly as he passed her.

Syd spun and hissed, "What's he doing here?"Then she half-laughed, hoping to distract her mother's keen nose for trouble. "Should I be looking for a lawyer?"

It didn't work. Letting the frown settle in, her mom studied Syd closely. "You're upset. What's the matter?"

"I...uh...are you dating him?" she whispered, shocked for no accountable reason, as she pointed, without turning to look, at the man leaning against his cop car.

A bemused look overtook the concern keeping her

mother questioning Syd instead of going – wherever it was she was going – with the Sheriff. "I guess I am. Crazy, isn't it?"

Shaking her head, she fought the denial pricking the back of her eyes. "Not crazy. Any man would be lucky to go out with you."

Her mom laughed. "Thanks for that. Now tell me what's wrong."

Syd hesitated, but couldn't hold it in, "Do you think a person gets a second chance?"

Unexpectedly, she was pulled into a fierce hug. "No, baby. I think we make our own second chances."

Letting her go, Lauren's thoughtful gaze settled for a moment on the cruiser before shifting back. "Is this about Ben?"

Syd jerked her chin down. "I don't know what to do. I made such a big mistake."

A mistake? God! Which one would that be? Sending him away in the first place, even though at the time she was trying to do the right thing? Leaving it too long to go after him? Or was it being fool enough to believe they had something special, that indefinable something that would see them through the rough patches? She'd been the first to cry uncle.

Gentle fingers stopped the desperate flow.

"What's done is done. Go with your heart, Syd. That's all any of us can do." Grabbing her wrist, Lauren tugged her along the walk. The Sheriff waited, arms across his chest, feet crossed at the ankles. "We're going to dinner. Come with us."

Sheriff Ford barely spared Syd a glance, instead smiling at her mom as they drew closer. She didn't need to be clobbered upside the head to see what was going on.

"I can't." She glanced at her watch. "I...told Ben I'd be at the JV game tonight."

A saucy grin curled her mother's mouth. "Go for it, sweetie. You only live once."

As the cruiser pulled away from the curb, her mother waving jauntily, Syd shook her head.

Go for it. What did that mean?

All the way to the football field, she argued with her mom's advice. Her predicament wasn't that simple. If her gamble didn't pay out, if things fell apart like the last time, it wasn't *her* heart that would take a painful tumble. There was Isabel to consider.

Having a second mother who couldn't be there every minute was not what the precious little girl needed. She needed someone whole; someone who would go the full nine yards with her. So did Ben. Syd's track record in that area was pathetic.

Sighing heavily, she parked the car. It wasn't hard to find Ben and Isabel. They were seated in the same bleachers as the last time. A skirmish was in progress. She felt Ben's eyes on her the minute she rounded the concession stand.

Her heart skipped a beat. *Be cool. Don't over react. You're feeling a little needy, is all.*

She climbed the bleachers, feeling lighter with every step that brought her closer to Ben.

His heated gaze traveled hungrily over her face, then down her very aware body. "Did you get your pictures?"

Suddenly at a loss for words, she nodded. Her hip brushed his as she sat next to him. Unadulterated awareness flamed across her skin from her head to her toes. God in heaven. She had to fight...this crazy attraction.

He angled toward her. Those disturbing eyes seeing straight through to her soul, roamed over her face before settling on her mouth, which went dry thanks to the blatant hunger he didn't bother hiding. Need grew into an uncontrollable ache low in her belly.

Desperate to keep from throwing herself, full body, onto the man, Syd cleared her throat and jerked free, her gaze landing beyond his wide shoulders.

She frowned. "Is that Kevin's little brother?"

Ben didn't take his eyes off her. "And his mother. Long story. Let's just say, the father is no longer in the picture. Kevin made sure of that."

The growl of approval in his voice drew her back. He was looking at her as if he couldn't wait to devour her. For a second, before she got control of herself, Syd wasn't sure she would stop him.

Images of them in his bed, his skillful hands exploring every inch of her body, almost had her devouring *him* right there. What had happened to her decision to keep as far from these explosive feelings as she possibly could?

The crowd roared. Isabel jumped to her feet and screamed. A touchdown, no doubt, Syd thought hazily.

Ben laced their fingers together. "I've decided to start a small press at the paper, to publish books like the one you're doing for Meredith."

His arched brows told her the truth. It was a bribe to lure her into staying. And God help her, against all good judgment and the unending argument she'd had with herself on the way over from her mom's, the temptation slipped unhindered into her heart. Staying in Rosewood might not be such a terrible idea.

Her cell rang. Syd fumbled for her phone.

"This is Sydney Marshall." She listened for a strung out minute, before responding. "I can be there on Friday."

Stunned by the call, and incredibly unsure how she felt about suddenly achieving everything she'd been working toward, she returned the phone to her pocket.

Ben watched her stoically. "Who was it?"

She kept her voice even. Why now, when her heart was getting other ideas? "Do you remember sending my resume to *Condé Nast?*

Suspicion bloomed in his gorgeous eyes. "Sure."

She pursed her lips, raising a brow at the unlikely timing. "Well, that was Ms. Batten from the HR Department. She wants me to come to New York. If the interview goes as well as she thinks it will, I've got a job. She wants me to fly in on the red eye Friday morning."

SIXTEEN

*B*en's heart sunk as he watched Kevin and the Junior Varsity squad score a victory for the home team. The crowd went wild, but all he could think about was Sydney and how she was about to leave Rosewood. Forever. Maybe not forever, she still had family and friends here, he reassured himself, but close enough.

He kept his eyes on Kevin. The kid didn't seem the worse for wear. The fight with his father hadn't done much damage. In fact, his step was light, as though a huge weight had lifted from his young shoulders. He was big for his age. Probably could take on a grown man, given the right incentive and that the betrayer had been drunker than a skunk. Watching your mother and little brother get beat would be enough to send anyone over the edge.

The same edge Ben stood on. He could feel it building inside as Sydney shifted beside him, cheering for the team as though she hadn't just given him the worst news ever. He should be happy that she'd gotten her job. And he would be. As soon as he let it sink in.

He'd planned to convince her to take a chance on them. That plan seemed juvenile now. Hiding his disappointment, he slowly rose to his feet at the game's end, joining the exuberant spectators around him.

And what was he to do about that whole forgiving herself part. He curled his hands into fists as the crowd started to disperse. What argument could he use to make her understand the past was done? That it couldn't be undone?

That was his problem. He had no argument. She would never forgive herself for not being there for her dad at the end. He totally understood. Would feel the same if he were in her shoes.

Shit. What a mess.

The only good news was she didn't seem as excited about the new job as he'd thought she would be. Unable to resist he put his hand to the small of her back and guided her down the bleachers. He felt the tremble that worked it's way through her body. A matching tremor reverberated in his gut.

"Have you eaten?"

Their feet hit the ground. She hesitated. "No."

"I'm having pizza delivered. Join us?"

"Yes! Please? Have pizza with us." Isabel was paying attention, bless her heart. Anything to keep Sydney with him for the remaining time left to them.

Nobody could resist his daughter when she was on her prettiest behavior. The woman taking over his life was no exception.

"Alright. Sure."

"Dad, can Kevin and his mom and Dillon come too?"

"Go ask them."

Isabel stood on her tippy-toes, depositing a sloppy kid kiss on his cheek. "You're the best."

His heart swelled. Now if he could convince Sydney of that, the only problem he'd have left would be how to make a long distance relationship work. He didn't know the answer; would have to cross that bridge when he came to it.

Reaching for her hand, he laced their fingers, thinking there was no time like the present to begin his last-ditch campaign to change her mind about them. "I'll order pizza on the way."

Her brows drew together in pretty confusion. He squeezed her hand; dropped a sizzling kiss on her parted lips, and wished he could tell her what he'd discovered in his heart. But not now. Not when the taste of surprise and straining desire inflamed his own growing fire. "Spend the night with me."

She pulled free, shook her head, but he didn't give her a chance to retreat too far. He retrieved her hand and kissed her fingertips, one at a time. "Follow me to the house?"

A hitch of her breath and jerk of her chin signaled capitulation. He let her escape then, gathered up Isabel, spent a few minutes with Kevin to make sure he and his family knew how to get to his place, then called in his order on the way to the car.

Sydney must have taken the long way around because she got there after he did; after his heart had climbed into his throat when he thought she might not show after all.

Kevin's mom parked her aging sedan at the curb.

Wanting to see what Sydney would see, Ben studied the craftsman critically as he unlocked the front door. He'd come to Rosewood to make a home for Isabel. As she hopped up the porch steps and dashed past him, dressed in pink and yellow instead of her usual standard black, he was flooded with sudden relief.

He'd accomplished what he set out to do; made a life for them in the town he'd grown up in. And his daughter was happy. If he could do all that, surely he could get one stubborn woman to see how good they were together, and what an incredible future they could have.

But she wasn't having any of it. He practically chased her through the rooms of his house, as she studiously avoided him, keeping the others between them.

Just before the pizza got there, Kevin nudged his mother. "Mr. Quincy, I didn't introduce you earlier at the school. This is my mom, Elizabeth Newman."

Keeping an eye on Sydney, Ben offered a hand. "Nice to meet you, Elizabeth." Kevin's mom was hesitant to return the courtesy, but finally did.

"Thank you for taking care of my boy." She spoke softly, as though she wasn't used to speaking out loud.

"He's a good kid."

She nodded, looked with pride at Kevin until the boy blurted.

"She needs a job."

"Kevin!" Appalled she drew away. "Don't pay him any mind. We're fine. I'm fine. I'll start looking for a job tomorrow."

"Pop's gone." Kevin's chin hitched. "I made him leave.

She needs a job," he persisted doggedly.

Sydney draw closer, her brows pulled together in concern. Ben's heartbeat settled. She cared about the people in their little town. She wouldn't be able to stay away long. That was a place to start anyway.

"Actually, I could use a receptionist at *The Gazette.* It would require some typing and computer skills, which can be learned, and someone who knows how to get along with people."

"Mom can get along with anybody," Kevin said, his tone derisive, but also hopeful.

Elizabeth batted him gently on the arm. "Shush, now."

Ben smiled at the kid before turning his attention back to the woman straightening her spine and raising her chin in perfect imitation of her son. "I took a typing class in high school, though I'm probably a little rusty, and I haven't used a computer much, except for when I go to the library. I can learn. I know I can."

"I'll need you to start tomorrow," Ben warned.

"I like to take Dillon to school."

"Hours would be Monday through Friday, while the boys are in school, say nine to three?"

Elizabeth Newman smile shyly, and the mouse turned into a sweet, gentle kitten. "Thank you, Mr. Quincy. You won't be sorry you hired me."

"It's Ben, and I'm sure I won't be."

He reached out to snag Sydney's arm as she turned away. *Oh no you don't. No more running.*

Her eyes swam with emotion. He pulled her away from the others into the kitchen, backing her against the counter.

Her hand fluttered to his chest, sending out spirals of heat. "That was a nice thing you did in there."

There was that word again. He shrugged, wondering if he dared indulged in the not so nice sentiment making him feel more alive than he had in years.

She daintily cleared her throat. "Look, I have to go. I have a lot to do before I get on that plane tomorrow night."

"You're leaving?"

Ben groaned. Isabel had followed them into the kitchen. There was too much to say to the woman in such a hurry to see the last of her hometown, but he stepped back, giving her space.

Sydney's desperate gaze slipped from his despair. "Um, yeah. I got a job in New York. I fly there for an interview tomorrow night."

Tears welled in Isabel's eyes. She stomped her foot. "That's dumb!" she shouted before running out of the room, the sound of her feet pounding on the stairs reverberating through the house.

The doorbell rang. Frustration thickened Ben's voice. "The pizza's here. You can't go yet."

"I have to."

The sorrow in her beautiful eyes punched him in the chest. He wasn't going to change her mind, he could see that now. Damn it! He was going to have to let her go.

He cursed soundly under his breath. "At least take some

with you."

She shook her head, and before he could stop her, Sydney Marshall, for the second time walked out of his house...and, as he'd known she would all along, out of his life.

~*~

She *wanted* to get out of Rosewood!

Even if it means leaving Ben...and Isabel?

She'd been living and breathing that dream for so long, how could she give it up?

Syd bottled her emotions, determined to take the practical route. There was no question. She wouldn't, couldn't fall into the trap of seeing herself playing the role of beloved wife and mother in Ben's little family.

She was on the verge of getting her dream job. *Go for it!* she admonished herself with her mother's words as she finished tying the lose ends at *The Gazette* by hitting send on the last of her emails to Ben.

She glanced around Meredith's office. Everything was in its proper place, just as it had been when she'd first taken over from the older woman after her stroke. All that was left was to meet her mother at Doc's, say her good-byes, and cop a ride to the airport.

The apartment she'd originally rented was gone, but she would find another one. She had an open ended round trip ticket. If everything went according to plan, it might be best to stay on in New York and get settled in, before coming back to arrange for her things.

Grabbing her backpack and suitcase, she locked the

house and drove across the river to Doc's place. His housekeeper let her in, taking her to the sitting room where laughter assaulted her even before Syd entered the quaintly decorated room.

"There she is." Meredith's bright eyes sought her out. "We've been waiting for you."

Four faces turned in her direction with varying degrees of speculation. Doc. Meredith. Her mother. The Sheriff – what was he doing here? They were all wondering if she was making another big mistake. She just knew it.

Well she wasn't. She remembered in vivid detail how shame had ripped through her when she'd run after Ben like a lovesick kid, only to be faced with the truth. She'd crawled back to Rosewood, her tail tucked between her legs, her heart shattered.

More heartache waited for her. She didn't ever want to live through that kind of pain again, knowing it was her own fault for believing she could make a fairy tale come true, when in fact, there was no such thing.

"I had some last minute things to take care of." That sounded more plausible than she'd had to keep busy so she didn't go after Ben like she had the last time.

Meredith patted the couch on her other side – the one that wasn't occupied by Doc Tucker, who sat surprisingly close, holding her hand between both of his.

Suddenly alert, she sat. Meredith and Doc had known each other practically all their lives. Syd had never noticed anything other than friendship between them.

"We have an announcement." Meredith sent a flirtatious smile over her shoulder. "David and I are getting married."

Syd glanced at her mother in disbelief. Lauren smiled, clearly happy for her friend.

"When?"

"Next month. And I want you to be my bridesmaid."

Syd was happy for Meredith and Doc. Damn it, she would be. As soon as she swallowed the lump clogging her throat. "Next month seems kind of soon."

Meredith cupped Syd's face. A sweet blush tinted her cheeks. "Life's too short. We don't want to waste a single minute of it."

Tears, the first real emotion Syd had allowed herself since walking out of Ben's house, flooded her eyes. Life *was* too short. Which was why a person should live it to the fullest, not chase after a man who had never been hers to begin with.

"You'll be in the wedding party?"

"I...would love to."

"Your mother is the Matron of Honor."

Lauren rose gracefully. "I hope you don't mind Ethan coming to the airport with us?"

"No!" Syd practically shouted before mentally grabbing her frantic self by the scruff of the neck. What was wrong with her? She all but had the job of her dreams right in the palms of her hands. She shoved the panic building in her chest aside and forced herself to be calm. "Of course not."

She swallowed hard. Her mother's nuptials would be next. She could see it in the way the Sheriff's hand settled on her mom's arm and how Lauren's eyes twinkled happily.

Ben and the way he looked at her the last time she'd seen him – like *he* hadn't wanted to waste another second – squeezed into her mind, but she didn't let him stay.

She had a plane to catch and a new life to get started. That hadn't change with Ben Quincy's return to Rosewood.

The ride through the dark to the Portland Airport wasn't short enough to suit Syd. Her mother drove way too sedately. She'd leaned forward to ask Lauren to go faster when the Sheriff twisted in the seat and eyed her with a considering look.

"New York's a long ways from home."

Yes, it was. But, was it far enough away from the guilt that had ridden her since the day her dad died without her at his bedside?

~*~

In the very early hours of Friday morning, Ben stood in his kitchen, guzzling coffee and staring out the window into the back yard. He hadn't slept at all. Why bother to try when all he would dream about was having Sydney there. With him.

His chest hurt like someone had taken a sled hammer and pounded on his heart until there was nothing but painful bruises left.

He looked at his watch for the millionth time. Her plane had landed in Newark three hours before – Rosewood time. Smacking his cup on the counter, hot liquid sloshed over the sides burning his fingers. He ignored the sting that came nowhere close to the ache searing his heart.

He'd let her dictate their future once – that had been his mistake. He'd been too full of pride and hurt feelings to step back and truly try to understand what she wasn't saying when she'd shoved him out of her life.

She'd wanted him to continue with his plans to go to the University of Chicago. He'd wanted to hold her hand through the horrific ordeal of watching her father die. He'd been too young to understand the intricate road of compromise. Instead he'd bolted.

Well, he wasn't that young man anymore. Since then he'd learned all about compromise, and this time he wasn't going to let Sydney be the one doing the bolting.

The shuffle of little slippers scuffed the floor behind him. When he turned, Isabel was rubbing her eyes with both fists, her hair a tangled mess falling to her slight shoulders.

"Why are you awake, kiddo? It's awfully early."

She came to lean against him and sniffed. "I couldn't sleep. I miss Sydney."

"Me too, baby."

He had no intention of moving his daughter out of Rosewood now that she'd finally grown comfortable in her new home, so his only option was to convince Sydney a long distance relationship could work.

And there was still the Clare Marsh column that would keep her connected to them. And he'd bet dollars to donuts, now that Isabel was happy, she would enjoy flying back and forth to the Big Apple and the woman he hoped to make her new mother.

There was no getting around it. Sydney Marshall was his heart, damn it. All he had to do was prove it to her. He would start with fresh flowers at Portland International Sunday morning.

He glanced at the time again. After he dropped Isabel off at school, he'd let Lauren know he'd be the one picking her daughter up at the airport.

He nudged Isabel toward the table. "How about French toast for breakfast?"

She shrugged.

He smiled at her less than enthusiastic response. That was okay, because he had a surprise in store for her. Come hell or high water, before he and Sydney got back to Rosewood, he would make every argument he could so she would see their future his way.

That was the plan anyway. He only hoped it worked.

~*~

Fingering the business card her new employer at *Condé Nast Traveler* had given her with the instruction to call him anytime during the weekend if she had any questions, Syd stared at the parasol lady clothed in the green patina of aged copper, who greeted visitors daily in Central Park.

The New York weather had turned chilly, but it didn't matter, because the interview had gone better than she'd thought it possibly could. She'd gotten everything she'd dreamed of in the job they offered; couldn't have asked for more.

She made a slow circle, taking in the luscious park, the

buildings that towered gracefully overhead, the people all going somewhere, the sound of traffic, horns blaring, the smell of city.

The perfect Prada bag hung from her shoulder. She'd found it on sale at a swank shop during her aimless wanderings. She loved New York. The sights. The sounds. The unabashed energy that permeated the city and it's natives.

Standing in the middle of her dream come true was when the truth drove over her like a runaway bus with no driver. She loved Rosewood...and Ben...more.

Her heartbeat skittered. Holy Mother – how had *that* happened? She'd come three-thousand miles to leave her guilt behind, and left it behind she must have, because all she could think about was getting back to the man she'd somehow come to love more than life itself.

She had to be with him; see the light of love he hadn't been able to hide the last time she'd been in his house. She wanted to be in his arms. Share the rest of her days with Ben, and every one of those days tell him what was in her heart. It'd been there all along, but she'd been too blind...and scared, if she was finally being honest, to look.

What was she going to do, she silently asked the parasol lady. The answer skipped gloriously into focus.

Pulling out her cell, she dialed the number on the card.

Sixteen nerve wracking hours later, her plane landed in Portland. Familiar flutters erupted in her stomach as her grip on the new Prada bag tightened. What if she'd read the signs wrong? What if Ben didn't want anything to do with her?

She grabbed her carry on from the overhead bin. It didn't matter. She had to give this – hopefully it was until-death-do-us-part – a shot. And if Ben wouldn't listen, she'd make him hear what she had to say.

Hurrying along the concourse, she emerged into the crowd waiting for debarking passengers. Searching for her mother, her eyes lighted on the man forcing her stomach to stumble. He carried a bouquet of bright wild flowers, his grey eyes shadowed with determination.

Heart pounding, she stopped an arm's reach away. Her words tripped over each other, but finally she got them out. "I took the job."

"We can make a long distance relationship work."

They spoke together.

A shaky laugh slipped past her lips. "If it's okay with you, we don't have to do it long distance."

Ben frowned. "But you just said–"

She took a tentative step toward the man she hoped would give her everything she'd forgotten she wanted. That he came with such a lovely daughter was icing on the cake. "I made a deal."

He closed the remaining distance. "What kind of deal?"

The deep timber of his voice circled Syd in a warmth that made her want more. She nodded at the flowers he held. "Are those for me?"

He removed them from reach, hiding them behind his back. "What kind of deal, Sydney."

She placed her hand over his heart, welcoming the storm spilling from his gorgeous eyes. "They want Clare Marsh. I convinced them, CM can live anywhere. I'm their new freelance contributor."

His frown deepened. He pulled her out of the flow of other arrivals. "Are you sure?"

"Oh yeah." She cradled his handsome face in both her hands and gave him a kiss he wouldn't soon forget.

Strong arms wrapped her in bands of steel. The scent of honeysuckle and daisies would stay with her forever.

Ben's free hand fisted in the thick fabric of her hoodie. "Marry me."

"Yes!" Her heart swelling, she smiled against his lips. "Can I have my flowers now?"

"That's not all you're going to get." His brows shooting up and down in sexy suggestion, he grabbed her hand and tugged. "Let's go home."

"I was hoping you'd say that."

Thank you for reading **The Return Of Benjamin Quincy!**
I hope you enjoyed it. If you did, please help other readers find this book by posting a review at any or all of your favorite review sites.

To find out about new books as soon as they become available, sign up for my newsletter, Su's News @ www.susanlute.com.

This book is lendable: send it to a friend you think might like it.

Find me on Facebook page @
http://www.facebook.com/pages/Susan-Lute/202040233153546

Pinterest http://www.pinterest.com/sidella/

Goodreads
https://www.goodreads.com/author/show/1252907.Susan_Lute

And Twitter https://twitter.com/SusanLute

Other Books by Susan Lute

A Girl Named Jane

Jane's Long March Home

The Marine's Christmas Proposal

The London Affair

The Broken Road

Dragon's Thief

A Fool For Love – A Sellwood Novella

The Girl Most Likely To: An Anthology

The Gift Of Christmas: An Anthology

Gifts From The Heart: An Anthology

Read on for a sneak preview of...

The London Affair

February 7

The worst thing that could happen to a woman who'd been in love for the better part of thirty-five years was to end up alone.

Well, not totally alone.

But alone as only a fifty-five year old woman could be when she's lost the very thing that made her life worthwhile.

Damn it, Jon!

Stella Carmichael eased the door of her Mount Tabor home closed and leaned against the hard wood, her head back, her eyes closed in a weariness she almost couldn't bear.

Almost.

When she opened her eyes, it was to an eerily unlit house, flooded with the gray of encroaching twilight. It smelled empty, if empty had a smell. Kind of a lingering echo of the earthy cologne Jon loved, but not really that either.

Her ears rang with the angry pulse of her blood.

Forcing herself to take one breath, then the next, she didn't notice when her purse dropped with a dull thud to the floor. Kicking off the shoes pinching her toes, she shrugged off her coat, dragged herself to the closet, looking for an empty hanger. But her limbs were too heavy to carry out the task of hanging up her coat.

And she would bet all that Jon had eagerly left behind - a sometimes contrary wife, his beautiful grown-up girls, the wayward granddaughter who was so much like him, the vintage home he'd helped restore, the job he coveted, their sometimes rocky, but for the most part, successful marriage - the feeling was never going to return to her arms and legs that felt like all the life had been sucked out of them.

Unable to bring herself to hang her coat next to the one he'd left behind, in a rare display of temper, she threw the offending garment in, slamming the door on the flying lump of black wool.

What were you thinking? her heavy heart railed. At him. At herself for not taking better care of what she'd had.

The phone rang once and the answering machine clicked on in the other room. "Stella, this is Dana Murphy." The doctor's voice echoed in the somber stillness. "I'm calling to see how you're doing. If you need anything at all, give me a call."

Dana had a women's clinic next door to Stella's office. They referred patients to each other and had been friends on a professional level for a long time.

What she needed, the doctor couldn't give her. Without bothering to turn on the lights, she made her way to the liquor cabinet her husband had meticulously made to fit into the pantry just off the kitchen.

She should sell the house and move on with her life, but thinking about it hurt too damn much.

It hurt that she couldn't sit folded in his strong arms

tonight, her back pressed close to his heartbeat as they watched their favorite romantic comedy on the big screen television he'd brought home on their last anniversary.

It hurt that she wouldn't wake up next to Jon tomorrow morning, his soft snoring brushing across her ear.

And it hurt that she couldn't smack him upside the head for the stunt he'd pulled, leaving her to watch the life they'd made together slip beyond her grasp.

For those reasons and those alone, she grabbed a full bottle of his favorite bourbon. Snatching a tumbler from the shelf above, she found her way by habit to the library that doubled as her office when she worked from home.

Stopping in the middle of the dark room, the bourbon in one shaking hand and tumbler in the other, clawing indignation mixed with her suffocating anguish. In the stillness where only overwhelming emotions had any life, the phone rang again. She didn't move to answer the annoying summons.

"Mom. I haven't heard from you in a few days. Call me as soon as you get this message."

When the demanding voice of her oldest daughter faded, the stifling silence engulfed Stella once more. Marching to her desk, she put the glass in the crook of her arm, opened the top drawer and searched the contents until she found the bottle of sleeping pills Dana had ordered for her.

Gripping the container until her knuckles turned painfully white, she caught her reflection in the mirror on the opposite side of the room. The woman who stared back had an arrogant tilt to her head as if she had the answer to every problem. She looked controlled. Clever. Like a woman who had plans for her life and was right on track.

Stella sneered. Foolish, foolish woman. Streaked blonde hair, not a strand out of place, curled serenely around her face, turning under at her shoulders. Intelligent, light brown eyes regarded her with pragmatic disinterest.

The woman didn't look like she'd been robbed of thirty-five years of a nearly perfect life.

Okay, so maybe they hadn't all been so perfect.

But, that didn't give Jon the right to casually throw away everything they'd built. On a whim. On a moment of stupid, illogic-

The silly twit staring at her had no clue she'd received a mortal blow; that her heart was breaking into bitter pieces, the gates of her usually controlled emotions about to break open and flood the entire room.

At least Stella didn't think she did until one lonely tear fell helplessly down her cheek.

Balancing the bourbon and pills close to her chest, she took a step toward the woman, struggling to pull the too heavy wedding set off her finger. In the silence of her ballooning misery, she wanted to throw the rings, but the best she could manage was to toss them against the mirror. They made a sharp ping when they hit and her voice cracked as if she hadn't used it in a very long time.

"Hi. My name is Stella. And I'm about to consume a shit-load of alcohol. Want to join me?"

What Readers are saying...

The Return Of Benjamin Quincy

RT Book Reviews ~ *"An engaging romance about how love can change dreams."*

"Susan Lute has created a charming novel filled with meddling relatives and friends, bad decisions, good decisions, flawed people, and passionate love. These are real people. No silly flippant girls or muscle bound men. These people have problems brought on because they thought they were doing what was best for the person they loved. Add an emotionally fragile 10 year old girl who needs them and you have this wonderful story." ~ Mindy K. Wall

"Susan Lute created a wonderful cast of characters and a charming town to help tell the story of finding your true happiness. I think each of us can find a little piece of Sydney in ourselves." ~ Cocktails and Books

"This was a highly enjoyable read. The story fit right into what I like to read in my contemporary romances." ~ Christina Snow

Jane's Long March Home

RT Book Reviews ~ *"A heartwarming [and] truly riveting story with beautiful characters and a plot you won't soon forget."*

Night Owl Reviews ~ *"A timely story that will appeal to those seeking a sweet story of finding yourself again."*

The London Affair

"Beautifully written, The London Affair by Susan Lute is the story of the inner workings of a complicated family and the hope of new beginnings. Read this book with a box of tissues." ~ Night Owl Reviews

"Susan Lute is a beautiful keeper of the human heart. She explores the soul and leaves the reader certain life is worth the journey." ~ Wendy Warren, 2-time recipient of the prestigious RITA Award

About The Author

Susan Lute is a multi-published, award-winning author of traditional and Indie books. She swears the best things in life come in unexpected packages. An ardent student of human nature, who loves ancient history, myth, and dragons. She doesn't remember thinking ... *someday I'll grow up to be a writer.* She writes whenever she can. In between she works as a Registered Nurse, reads, gardens, loves to travel, and work on remodeling her house. She lives in the Pacific Northwest with her husband of many years. Currently she's working on the next novel in her Dragonkind Chronicles, and because she has too much curiosity and a short attention span, is writing a new mainstream romance.